WISH I
WEREN'T HERE

•

Sandra D. Bricker

AVALON BOOKS
NEW YORK

PRINTED IN THE UNITED STATES OF AMERICA
ON ACID-FREE PAPER
BY HADDON CRAFTSMEN, BLOOMSBURG, PENNSYLVANIA

FOR JEMELLE:
Cheerleader, Coach, Chef, Chauffer,
Psychiatrist, and Role Model.

And FOR DIANE:
Nurse, Personal Shopper, Housekeeper,
Jokester, and Therapist.

The only two women on earth
who could somehow manage
to make even *CANCER* bearable.
Thank you for hanging in there
when you had no good reason to do it.
You're both even more fabulous
on this side of the monster.
I love you.

Thanks, as always, to Erin Cartwright-Niumata.
You know how to keep a writer going.
Thank you for your sass and your encouragement.

And special thanks to a critique partner I had
once upon a time.
Your input, patience and talent
helped me walk this book through a lot of changes.

Chapter One

"How long has it actually been since you've had a date?"

Vic paused over the signature line of the contract before her, the pen poised in the air as if she'd recently made contact with the sizzling electrodes of a stun gun. Drawing air into her lungs at a pace more leisurely than was customary, she raised her eyes and stared at her assistant.

"I beg your pardon?"

"Well, I was reading an article in this month's issue of *Cosmo*—" the moptop girl began.

"That's what I like about you, Krissy. The way you keep things so scientific. Tell me, were you reading this article on company time?"

"—and it says one of the top causes of stress in the workplace stems from women who aren't being fulfilled romantically. And I got to thinking that, well, Richard's been gone, what, a year now?"

"Has it been that long?" Vic asked as she ignored the sudden, excruciating pinch at the mention of Richard's name and pretended to return her attention to the paperwork at hand.

"At least," Krissy continued. "And, well, it got me to thinking that maybe that's your problem."

"What do you mean you've fallen in love with another woman? When did you have the time? All you ever do is work, Richard! When could you have met and courted and fallen in love with someone else?"

Vic painstakingly signed her name to the contract in front of her, forcing the replay of her final conversation with Richard back down where she'd left it eleven months prior, securely bound and gagged at the pit of her stomach.

"At least consider the fact that I might be making a valid point," Krissy went on. "I'm worried about you, Boss. Is that so terrible?"

Placing the pen back into the brass well, Vic made sure to blink back the mist of emotion before she raised her eyes and looked sternly at her assistant. It was a mask she'd developed over the last year of her life, and she could wear it confidently now, like a fistful of aces at a poker game.

"You know, you really could be on to something here, Krissy."

"Really?" The young woman replied hopefully, then tossed her head in a way that made her bowl of golden curls dance around her face.

"Yes. Really. I mean, I do have a lot of frustration."

"This is what I was thinking!"

"It's just been glaring me in the face all this time."

"Sometimes you just need someone to point out the obvious, Vic. Sometimes all it takes—"

"And I have you to thank for the answer."

"Well, it was actually *Cosmo* that made me think of it. Do you want me to get you the magazine? If you read the article—"

"No, no," she said with a sigh. "I don't need to read the magazine to glean the brilliance of your idea. It's genius, in fact."

Krissy deflated suddenly, her brown eyes narrowing skeptically.

"So I guess . . . Yes. I think we're on to something here . . . Krissy, you're fired."

"I should have seen that coming," she commented softly, scooping up the paperwork on her boss's desk and clicking her tongue in disappointment. "I was just trying to help."

"You know what would really help?" Vic asked her as she leaned back into the soft leather chair and propped her feet on the open desk drawer.

"No," Krissy replied, shifting her weight to one foot, seemingly preparing for the zinger that was likely to follow. "What?"

"You could . . . *do your job.*"

"Okay—"

"No, really," Vic continued excitedly. "You could take these contracts down to Legal, and then you could order my lunch before you come back to your desk and type up that mountain of correspondence I dictated to you this morning. And then, you know what you could do?"

"All right, all right," Krissy said, silencing her with the frantic wave of her arm. "I can see where this is headed. I've got your point."

"Oh good."

Krissy paused at the door and looked back at her boss. "You know, those test results from your physical are no joke, Vic. Your blood pressure is sky-high, and your cholesterol levels are almost as bad."

Vic snapped open the small leather case before her and produced a cigarette. She slipped it between her lips as she placed the elegant gold lighter into her fist.

"And you need to quit that too. Mr. Marchant as much as said so, didn't he?"

Vic narrowed her eyes at Krissy and stared her down. "Do you know how you can save your job, Krissy?"

"By ordering your lunch and minding my own business."

"Very good. You're hired again, on a temporary basis. Now let's see if you can last through the afternoon without breaching the boundaries of your employment here, shall we?"

"Can I say just one more thing?"

Vic arched a brow and waited.

"This is a no smoking building. If you set off the alarm and the sprinklers ruin your Chanel, there's not a dry cleaner in town who will be able to have it ready for your four o'clock meeting with Mason Foods."

"Fair enough," Vic replied, blowing a cloud of smoke in Krissy's general direction.

Without another word, her assistant seemed to roll around the jamb, and then disappeared on the other side of the door before closing it gently.

Vic leaned her head back into the burgundy leather, closed her eyes, and released a long, weary sigh. Firing Krissy had become a weekly event, and their banter had become a sort of game that she depended upon. In that moment of silence, Vic thanked God for such a wonderful assistant; one who took her as she was on a daily basis, in good spirits or bad, and who always seemed to bounce back with more affection and respect for her than she'd had before. The truth was Vic didn't know what she would ever do without Krissy.

When she opened her eyes again, her gaze rested on the ceiling and an unceremonial grin wound its way over her entire face. She'd disconnected the smoke alarm herself just that morning. Nothing to worry about. Her 4:00 P.M. meeting would find her neatly dry and pressed, if just the slightest bit tainted by the distant scent of tobacco.

Now back to work.

Vic pivoted around to the computer screen, taking one last puff from her cigarette before she began tapping at the keys before her.

I still have three hours before the meeting. Trenton will be so dazzled by this campaign, he'll spread out the offer to become the company's new Creative Director right at my feet. After all, she thought somewhat bitterly, *this is what I do best.*

"Krissy, call Dave in the art department, will you?" she called out in the general direction of the phone while pressing the intercom button. "I need that artwork by three."

"He knows. You told him this morning," she returned.

"Tell him again. Krissy?"

"I'll tell him again."

"And what about that email from the client? Did we get the stats?"

"I haven't checked your incoming emails yet, but if it came, it will be in the downloaded incoming mail file on your desktop."

"Oh, and Krissy?"

"Ham and swiss on rye with extra chips and two pickles," her assistant returned instinctively. "It should be delivered any minute."

How does she do that?

"Oh! And—"

"Dr. Pepper, extra ice."

"Thank you, Krissy," she sang only slightly patronizingly.

"Welcome, Miss Townsend," her assistant returned in a matching tone.

The presentation couldn't have gone better, but Vic could have done without that stranger in the corner distracting her.

Who is this guy? she found herself thinking again and again, trying to remain focused on the twosome she knew to be the all-important clients from Mason Foods. And focused also, of course, on her stepfather, Trenton Marchant, who presided over the ordeal like an emperor surveying his kingdom from the throne at the head of the conference table.

"We'll be in touch," one of the clients promised as the two disappeared into the hall, and she knew he meant it. The presentation was brilliant, even if she did say so herself.

"I look forward to it," Vic returned, closing the door behind them.

Turning to face Marchant, her eyes were once more drawn instead to the golden-haired visitor in the corner. The denim of his jeans was dark enough to look business-appropriate beneath a starched white shirt and topped off with a black sport coat. Emerald green eyes seemed to shimmer at her as the chiseled square of his jaw shifted and one corner of his mouth rose into a lopsided smile.

"Well," Vic spouted, peeling her eyes away from the stranger and letting them rest on Marchant. "I'd say that went very well."

"I knew it would," he returned, but the rare validation Marchant bestowed paled in comparison to the magnetic pull of the stranger.

"Have we met?" Vic couldn't help asking.

"Not yet," he replied in a voice as smooth as yesterday's ice cream.

"Allow me to introduce Andrew Nolan," Marchant supplied. "Drew, my stepdaughter, Victoria Townsend."

The voltage was unmistakable when their palms met, and Vic uncharacteristically withdrew first.

"A pleasure," he told her.

"Likewise."

"Drew is Fisher Nolan's boy," Marchant explained, and Vic marveled at the lack of resemblance between her stepfather's former business partner and the suntanned prince who looked very much like he'd recently stepped from the pages of a New Age fairy tale.

"Your father and Trenton were in the service together," she

remarked, wishing he would fix his gaze elsewhere. His eyes seemed to press in on her like a steam iron.

"So they were."

"How is your father?"

"He passed away last year," Drew replied, and regret crowded Vic's throat.

"I'm sorry."

"Thank you."

"Why don't we all sit down for a few minutes," Trenton suggested, and Vic was grateful for the reprieve.

She slipped down into the chair she'd occupied during the presentation, and then took a long draw from the half-empty glass of water before her.

"Fisher sold off most of the enterprises we cooked up together before parting company back in '89," her stepfather told her as he sat down at the head of the table, signaling Drew to the chair at his left. "And he spent his final years doing what he loved best. Batting a little white ball around green hills and sand traps. I never did understand his penchant for the game."

"Dad used to say that golf is an acquired taste," Drew grinned at the older man. "Like clams."

"I never learned to appreciate those either. Your father and I were about as different as two men could ever have been."

"Ah, but there's a certain beauty in opposition," Drew replied with half a shrug, then turned his green-tinted gaze back on Vic. "Wouldn't you say, Miss Townsend?"

What did he mean by that?

"I suppose there is," she conceded.

"I'm happy to hear you say that, my dear," Trenton added. "Because opposition is what I'd like to speak to you about."

"Oh?"

Vic looked from Marchant to Drew and back again. What was going on here?

A sudden shudder of revelation coursed through her at that moment, and Vic leaned forward to the walnut table.

"What is Mr. Nolan doing here, Trenton?"

"That's my stepdaughter, Andrew," Marchant smiled. "She gets straight to the point."

"I can see that."

"So why don't you do the same," she suggested seriously. "Let's get right to the point. Does this little meeting have anything to do with the appointment of our new creative director?"

"Yes, I suppose it does."

She'd heard the rumors, but she'd discounted them, believing Trenton was enough of a businessman at heart to know better than to award the promotion to anyone else, much less some stranger from outside the company.

Calm down, Vic ordered herself firmly. *Maybe you're jumping to conclusions. Just settle down and let him get to it.*

"Since the announcement is scheduled for tomorrow morning," she said, "I assume you've made your decision."

"Yes, Victoria. I have."

"And are you planning to give me a preview, or do I have to wait along with everyone else in the company?"

"I know how badly you want this appointment," Trenton began, and Vic saw the writing on the wall as clearly as if he'd hired a band of graffiti artists to storm the gates.

"Trenton, you've got to be joking."

"I'm sorry, Victoria, I really am. But if you'll just hear me out—"

"You know good and well that I'm the right choice for that job!" she exploded, rising to her feet with the sheer impact of it. "I've worked my fanny off for this company. Nobody knows how to sell a product like I do. Look at the figures! Look at the accounts we've satisfied over the last year alone!"

"I'm not disputing your abilities, my dear."

"Don't do that," she seethed. "Don't call me *dear* as if I'm sixteen again, asking you for my first car. I've more than proven myself in the nine years I've worked here. You started me out at the bottom, Trenton. You've never shown me one bit of favoritism because I happened to be the daughter of the woman you married. I've put blood, sweat, and tears into this place and worked eighteen-hour days for months at a time—"

"Which is precisely my point."

"I've juggled multi-million dollar campaigns for you, Trenton. And made you almost as many dollars to tuck away in your own pocket! And now, just when we come to the point where you can reward me the same way you would reward any employee who has worked this hard for you, you . . . you . . . You toss me aside?"

"Victoria, I assure you—"

"No!" she exclaimed, slamming both fists to the table and leaning across it toward him. "I don't want your assurances, Trenton. I want that job."

"Sit down," he said softly, but she made no move to back down. "I said," he continued, raising the level of his voice just enough to be heard above the rush of adrenalin pounding through her body, "sit down."

Vic felt as if she was blinking for the first time in hours, and she swallowed hard around the lump in her throat before slipping into the chair behind her.

"Look, I'm sorry," she told him sincerely. "But I've worked very hard for you."

"Yes, you have," he conceded. "Too hard, in fact."

"And you repay me by bringing in the son of an old war buddy to do the job that I'm clearly the most qualified for?"

"No, that's—" Drew interjected.

"What experience does he have that you would hand over a creative team the size of ours to him?" she continued. "Look at him! He looks like one of the male models we would hire for a sportswear layout!"

The model grimaced at her before he said, "If I could just . . . say . . . something—"

"What do you know about advertising?" she asked him incredulously. "What could you possibly bring to the table of a company the size of Marchant?"

"Well, that's why I'm here. To learn—"

"To learn!" she blasted back. "You're going to put him into the highest position in the company so that he can *learn?* Trenton, have you lost your mind? Is that it? Have you gone absolutely out of your ever-loving mind?"

Marchant's eyes narrowed at her in a way she'd seldom seen in the twenty-some years since he'd come into her life, and then he rose to his feet, as calm and mellow as milk in a glass.

"Andrew," he stated, "will you excuse us for a moment?"

"Certainly."

Vic glared at him as Drew moved past her and made his exit. When she looked back at Trenton, he hadn't flinched. It was as if he were standing there posing for a portrait. When he finally parted his lips to speak, she felt certain that several minutes had passed.

"I loved your mother, Victoria."

Vic took a deep breath and released it very slowly before replying. "Yes, I know you did."

"When she died five years ago, I wasn't sure I could find the will to go on."

"I understand the feeling."

"She had become my entire life. And because she loved you so deeply, you became a part of that circle."

"I know."

"You weren't the easiest child in the world, certainly you know that. And you gave me a hard time in the beginning."

"Is that what this is, Trenton? Payback?"

Her glower faded in the light of the unexpected smile that crept up over his face in response.

"Payback," he repeated, and then paused thoughtfully. "I suppose it is, in a way you couldn't understand."

Butterflies swarmed in her stomach, and a craving for nicotine pinched at every flutter.

"The one and only concern your sweet mother had when she knew the cancer was going to win out," he continued, "was about you."

A subtle wave of emotion crested in her eyes, and Vic cringed at the disclosure.

"She never felt that Richard was the right man for you. Did you know that?"

Vic shrugged half-heartedly. She'd known it deep down, but the actual words had never been exchanged.

"He wasn't a bad man," he expounded, "he just wasn't the right one for you. He brought out all of the tangible aspects of your personality, but never the more spiritual ones. And that concerned your mother more than she was able to express to you."

Vic didn't speak, but she cocked her head slightly, curious as to the implications of this sudden revelation.

"You are a very hard worker, Victoria, a committed, dedicated employee to this company, and you've climbed its walls with sheer determination and talent. I'm very proud of you for that."

"Th-thank you."

"I've seen you emerge from a simple apprentice to a first-rate corporate artisan. You would make a wonderful creative director."

Hope bubbled up inside of her, making its way from the depth of her soul right to the arch of her brows. That is, until she looked into Trenton's eyes, where she discerned honest regret.

"But?" she prodded.

"Have you read the physician's report from your physical? Your blood pressure and cholesterol—"

"Those are just numbers, Trenton."

"But you are not, Victoria. You are not just a number. Or a mere Marchant employee. You are my stepdaughter. The only daughter of the only woman I have ever loved."

"What are you saying?"

"I'm saying I'm worried about you. Those numbers, as you call them, should have been a wake-up call to you. They certainly were to me. You eat, sleep, and breathe your job, Victoria."

What is this, some kind of long-term group intervention? First Krissy, now Trenton?

Suddenly, a different realization started to dawn, like an annoying cloud of descending gnats, and Vic leaned forward curiously.

"So . . . what? You brought the son of your old friend into town so that I would . . . *get a life?* Is that it? You've chosen this Andrew Nolan for me?"

"Certainly not," he said on a chuckle. "I wouldn't presume to choose a man for you, any more than your mother would have been so brazen as to express her reservations about your choice in Richard."

"Let's cut to the chase then, Trenton. What's he doing here?"

"Andrew runs Romantic Overtures, the last company that

Fisher and I financed together, and the one company his father didn't sell off before he retired. The business has hit a bit of a snag. It's in trouble, and Andrew has come to me for help in saving it."

"What does that have to do with the director's appointment?"

"In regard to you, it has everything to do with it."

"I don't understand."

"Victoria, I'm going to give you that position you want so badly."

"You are?" She brightened, and then realization fell on her hope like a wet cloak. "What's the catch?"

"You're a very insightful woman," he congratulated her. "And once again, your instincts are right on target."

Why do I feel like I'm about to be presented with the key to the executive washroom in my own lavish office somewhere in Iceland?

"You will be Marchant Media's creative director, Victoria," Trenton stated. "And you will start six months from today."

"Six months . . ."

"And in between now and then, you will be exclusively assigned to the task of overhauling Andrew's business. In St. Petersburg, Florida."

"I don't quite . . . I don't understand."

"I want you to move to Florida, Victoria. I want you to put that brilliant creative mind to work on saving that boy's business. And in your off hours, I want you to get some fresh air and sunshine. I want you to eat right and get some exercise. In short, Victoria, I want you to get yourself healthy, in body and spirit."

"In . . . Florida?"

"I've given this a great deal of thought, and it's what your mother would want for you. I know it is."

"Trenton, I can't move to Florida. I'm just not a Florida kind of girl. This is me! Victoria Townsend! I'm a New Yorker. I bleed the Hudson River, Trenton."

"Look at it as an extended vacation," he suggested.

"But *Florida*. That's where old people go to die! There are bugs the size of subway cars in Florida. And do you watch the news? People are eaten by alligators on a regular basis there.

And the weather! I'll be cooked down to nothing in that humidity. I . . . I can't move to *Florida!*"

"For six months," he reminded her. "And then you'll come back here, have another physical and, God willing—or doctors willing—you will then be ready to take your rightful place as creative director of Marchant Media, Inc."

Vic was stunned. When she found her voice again, it came out in a raspy little squeak. "This is outrageous."

"No," Trenton stated seriously, "this is your chance. You do as I ask, and you'll have what you say you truly want."

"But . . . *Florida?*" Vic paused and massaged her aching head vigorously with both hands. "Can't I work on the account from here?"

"Andrew is prepared to make radical changes in his business as needed to build it into something profitable. He's going to need you there. And I think he has a lot he can teach you in turn about relaxing, Victoria."

"From the looks of him, I'm sure he does," she replied sarcastically. "Did you see that tan and that hair, Trenton? It's no wonder his business is in trouble. He probably spends all his days dodging sharks from his surf board!"

"Well then, you can balance one another out. He'll teach you to relax, and you'll teach him how to build a business."

I'll teach him something, all right. I'll teach him how to be sorry he played a role in putting this hare-brained idea into my stepfather's head!

"And make no mistake, Victoria. I want you to give this your all. If you do not come back here in six months' time with a suntanned, relaxed smile on that pretty face of yours, and blood pressure readings to match, the door to the creative director's office is going to be engraved with someone else's name."

Vic narrowed her eyes at Trenton, weighing the threat against the seriousness of his expression.

"This is blackmail, you know."

"I'm aware of that."

"You're a horrible man."

"Yes. But a loving stepfather."

"Ah, Trenton," she grimaced. "Bite me."

Chapter Two

Drew supposed that the finely-creased tan trousers and sleeveless white sweater Vic donned when she appeared in the terminal were her best stab at casual, but he wanted to let out a laugh just the same. Summer in Florida was no place for a sweater, sleeveless or not!

Balancing a smart leather briefcase under her arm, she approached him and extended her hand.

"Mr. Nolan. Good to see you again."

She was all business, just as Trent had warned him.

"Drew," he told her. "Can I take your briefcase for you?"

"Thank you, but I'm quite capable of carrying it myself," she declared. "Which way to baggage?"

"There's a tram," he said, leading the way. "Do I call you Victoria? Or do you go by something simpler? Vicki?"

"Vic," she stated, and then stepped onboard.

"Vic."

Tampa International Airport was large by southern standards, but Drew imagined it was a walk through the park for Victoria Townsend. His experience at Kennedy Airport, on the other hand, had been nothing short of exasperating.

"You wait here," he told her once they'd collected her bags. "I'll go get the car."

"I can walk to it," she replied, and he decided not to argue. This was a woman with whom it was probably wise to choose one's battles.

"Okay, but it's a scorcher today."

He tried not to look, but he couldn't manage to resist. And she didn't let him down when the elevator doors flew open and the large, wet greeting of ninety-two-degree heat smacked into her like a roller derby warrior. Her beautiful, composed face melted down into complete displeasure, and the barely-audible groan that accompanied it said more than words ever could have.

"Welcome to Florida," he quipped, tugging at the handle of her largest bag and wheeling it along behind him.

13

He'd parked on the second level, and he had her bag into the trunk of his convertible Mustang before she finally joined him there, panting slightly.

"Let me get that," he said, levering the other two bags over the edge of the trunk and tossing it shut.

She glanced at his apple-red car with disdain before sliding down into the passenger seat and fastening the buckle. Okay, the car was old, and not exactly in cherry condition, but he loved that car. Vic, on the other hand, clearly did not.

"Did you want me to put up the top?" he asked politely, hoping she wouldn't.

"No," she replied finally. "I guess this will be fine. Mind if I smoke? It was a long flight without a cigarette."

She lit up before he could reply, and the streams of smoke that floated out into the air just added to Drew's proud pleasure in owning the convertible.

"Do you want to stop off for lunch?"

"No," she answered, sucking up a lungful of smoke and blowing it into the air between them. "I'd like to see where I'll be living and try to settle in."

"All right."

"Trenton tells me there are apartments near the office complex?"

"Well, there are apartments above the office," he corrected. "Two of them. It's pretty small, but you can see the water from your living room window."

"Oh."

"I think you'll like it."

"I'm sure it will suffice. It's only six months out of my life, after all."

Drew cast her a look that she didn't seem to notice. What a joy of a summer this was going to be! His thoughts dissolved when he was caught on the check by a cascading ash.

"You might want to put that out when we get to the bridge. It gets pretty windy on the water."

She seemed to consider his suggestion, then shrugged her slender shoulders before tugging open the ashtray.

"Oh," she remarked, and he looked down to find her digging

the spare change out of the metal compartment before stamping out the butt and flicking it inside the once-pristine tray. "Here."

He received the handful of coins and, after a moment's consideration, adjusted to deposit them into the pocket of his brown cotton shorts.

Vic continued the uphill battle against her hair, which flapped its shiny black locks at her face in unrelenting assault. Finally, Drew leaned across her and popped open the glove compartment, producing a terrycloth band he kept there for Penelope.

"This might help," he said, extending it toward her, and then he watched as Vic combed through her hair with long, slender fingers and confined it to a ponytail so short at the back of her head that it seemed to be pointing the way back home.

"Yes. Thank you."

Traffic was light across the Howard Frankland Bridge, almost as light as the conversation while they drove along. Drew would turn to look at her every now and again, but each time her face seemed utterly frozen in that annoyingly poised stance, her chin slanted upright, and that tiny upturned nose stuck in the air like she was the Queen of England.

He glanced over at her again to find that Vic seemed to soften at the sight of the water, squinting as she looked off into the horizon, and Drew followed her gaze for an instant in an effort to see his world through the crystal blue eyes of this irritating newcomer.

Small caps of foam topped blue-green ripples that shimmered at the touch of golden fingers of sunlight. In the distance, sailboats and jet skis danced a perfectly choreographed polonaise across the surface of the water, and the palm trees at the shoreline were silhouetted against the reflection, keeping precise rhythmic time in their dance.

"I'll bet I can read your mind," Drew said softly, casting Vic an amiable smile.

"Oh?" she asked him, placing sunglasses on her face and depriving him of the view of her amazing blue eyes.

"You were thinking what a beautiful place this is."

"Well, actually," she began, then turned her head away from

him, "I was thinking I can't believe I have to spend the next six months in a tropical sauna. I'm really going to have to go shopping for a whole new wardrobe."

Drew was silent for a long moment. Few people surprised him any more, but this woman was a true piece of work.

"Right," he returned with a chuckle. "That's what I meant."

"Then I guess you really could read my mind," she quipped.

"Yeah. I never miss. It's a gift."

Vic could hardly believe her eyes. She lowered her sunglasses to the bridge of her nose and took another look.

"This is it?"

The office complex she'd anticipated melted away like a waxen mirage. She found herself faced instead with the reality of an old two-story building, moderately charming in a Tennessee Williams sort of way, but certainly not somewhere she would eagerly have chosen to spend the next six months of her life. But then she hadn't really been given a choice, had she?

"Home, sweet home," Drew announced as he climbed out of the car, opening his arms proudly as if he expected her to swoon at the very sight.

"It certainly is."

Vic rounded the car and waited at the back while Drew opened the trunk. Just as she was about to reach inside for one of her bags, a horrible growl drew her attention to the side of the building.

"Oh my!" she cried as she spotted it: a seething black Australian Shepherd, which let loose a cacophony of high-pitched barks that seemed to be aimed directly at her.

"Quiet, Louie," Drew demanded, but Louie apparently had dropped out of the Doggie School of Obedience before completing his studies. "Inside. Now!"

Vic was caught off guard and jumped at the command, ready to make her way quickly toward the door.

"Not you," Drew added softly. "I meant him."

"Oh, of course."

As the twosome approached the steps to the front porch, the dog's incessant barking neither ceased nor curtailed.

"He's really a pussycat," Drew told her. "He just has the lungs of a lion."

"And the teeth."

The dog was nearly spitting at her as he continued his tirade, but he made no move to block her from entering through the front door Drew opened for her. Taking timid steps, Vic moved past the animal and walked inside. To her chagrin, Louie was allowed to follow.

"Louie, can it!"

The dog quieted down to a dull growl for a few moments, but then began barking full force once more.

"He won't always be this noisy," Drew promised. "Once he gets to know you and the two of you become friends, your presence will be old news."

Then I'd better get used to the barking, Vic warned herself. *This dog and I are never going to become friends.*

"Well, this is the office," he pointed out with little pomp and circumstance. "There's a small kitchen back there. And a bathroom and conference room through there."

"And my living quarters?"

"Up the outside stairs," he told her.

With a cautious glance toward the dog, she stepped lightly back out the door. It was a clumsy trip up the concrete stairs with her share of the bulky luggage in tow, but Vic followed Drew on the ascent. When he stopped at the top, she nearly rammed face-first into his derriere.

"Ohhh," she squealed, stopping short by only a half inch or so.

"Sorry. I was checking to see if you needed any help."

"I can manage," she returned coolly. "Which way from here?"

Drew led the way down a narrow walkway to the first door and jiggled a key into the lock. The dog ran through the door the moment it opened.

"It's not much," he announced as they followed.

No, it certainly isn't.

"I had been renting it out to a college student who's been helping me out in the office for a while," he continued, and she could scarcely hear him over the latest chorus of resistance from his faithful companion, Louie. "But when Trent suggested you come down and work with me onsite—"

"Yes," she cut him off. "I understand."

"It looks a little stark with all of Tiffany's things moved out, but I'm sure you'll give it your own personal touches."

Tiffany? He was renting to a college girl named Tiffany?

Visions of flowing blonde hair and fleshy curves came instantly to mind.

"It's only temporary," she told him. "It will suffice."

"O-kay," he snapped. "I've stocked the fridge with a few essentials. There are linens in the closet in the hall. The phone is turned on. And I'll be down the landing if you need me."

"What?" she asked, stopping him short. "You'll be where?"

"I live next door."

"Oh. I see. I hadn't realized . . ."

"Yep," he returned. "Welcome to the neighborhood. Louie!"

And with that, he and the beast that followed him were gone, their exit punctuated by the slight slam of the door.

Vic dropped her briefcase on the arm of an overstuffed wingback chair and crossed to the window, pulling open the cotton drapes. Behind the building was a small street, bordered on the opposite side by several low structures which seemed to be apartment buildings and storefronts. Beyond them, there it was again, that despicable salt-heavy surf. There certainly was a lot of it.

Oh, how she longed for a subway ride across town just then, nothing more outdoorsy to occupy her thoughts than the Jamaican scene silk-screened to the front of the T-shirt worn by a fellow commuter.

Entering the miniscule kitchen, she eased open the refrigerator door and examined the contents. Eggs, milk, a block of cheese and some cartons of yogurt. A variety of juices dotted the door shelf along with several bottles of water; a lonely loaf of whole grain bread sat on the otherwise barren bottom shelf. A clump of leafy green lettuce peered up at her from the translucent compartment beneath it, and an array of produce bobbed around like disembodied heads when she slid open the drawer. Clunking it shut, she noticed a wire basket hanging over the sink that was brimming with oranges, apples and several greenish bananas. She would have to begin assembling takeout menus sometime very soon or she would definitely starve.

The bedroom was little more than a closet, only large enough for a small single bed and a four-drawer maple chest. Sheer white curtains revealed a large sliding glass door that led to a tiny balcony, barely big enough to hold the lounge chair and plastic table that was nestled into the space. The adjoining bathroom was an eerie shade of green with an old claw-footed tub, a toilet, and a small vanity. The tiny window beyond the tub was set high into the wall and displayed a colorful stained glass rendition of an awkward aquarium of swimming fish.

"Trenton," she said aloud, "what have you done to me?"

Vic set about the task of unpacking, which took under an hour to complete, and then moved on to the final chore of settling the fresh pharmaceutical bottles on the kitchen counter next to the coffee pot.

"Accupril," she read aloud distastefully, smacking the third and final bottle to the tile.

The hair at the back of her neck stood on end as she stared at it. She was too young to be worrying about such things as high blood pressure!

Lighting up a cigarette, she gazed out the kitchen window and wondered if Krissy had remembered to send the weekly report down to Accounting that morning.

"Well, what's she like?"

"A little like you'd imagine a New York ad exec to be, I guess. Only mix in a little constipation, no life outside of the office, and a dash of evil incarnate."

"Come on, Drew," Penelope urged him. "Paint me a picture here."

Drew grinned, cradling the telephone to his ear with his shoulder while cracking open a bottle of fruit juice.

"She looks remarkably like Courteney Cox," he said carefully. "In the first season of *Friends*. Before David Arquette."

"She's beautiful then."

"Yes, she's beautiful. Brilliant blue eyes, shoulder-length black hair, sort of layered and natural, and she's small and shapely . . . And then you get a centimeter deeper."

"What then?"

"A chain-smoking, arrogant dragoness with the personality of an arthritic pit bull."

"She can't be all that bad," Penelope prodded hopefully. "There's got to be more to her than that."

"Oh yeah, I'm sure there is. My guess is it only gets worse."

"Well, I'm sorry, sweetie. But maybe she's just mean enough to know what to do to get your business back on track."

"Or die trying, I'd say," he replied, and then took a long swig from the bottle of juice. "If there's one thing Victoria Townsend is all about, she's all about business."

"Then that's a good thing."

"Always accentuating the positive, aren't you, Pen?"

A wave of heat moved over him as Drew turned and found himself staring into Victoria Townsend's disapproving face.

"Uh, Pen? I've got to go. I'll talk to you later, okay?"

"All right then. Are we still on for the beach?"

"Sunset. Be there."

"I'll be there. You be there."

"Uh," he muttered as he turned away. "Gotta go, see ya."

Drew replaced the cordless phone on its nest, then turned back sheepishly.

"What can I do for you?" he asked innocently.

"If I can tear you away from your love life, I'd like to get a look at your client files."

Love life? Pen was about as far from being part of Drew's nonexistent love life as a woman could come. She was more of a maternal figure, really; wearing the guise of best friend. She'd been his professor for one class at the university, and he'd been amused by her slight Jamaican accent and the easy, warm humor she possessed. Her class had been a challenge he'd enjoyed, and Drew and Pen had been the best of friends ever since.

"Services rendered over the last two quarters," the pit bull was saying. "Follow-up reports on quality of service. A mission statement for the company if you have it handy. And is there an office I can occupy for some privacy? If not, the conference room will do. I assume there's a phone line at my disposal?"

Drew looked at her curiously for a moment, and then she met his gaze with one of her own; one which wordlessly spoke to him in clear and distinct resonance: *What part of the English language do you not understand, you dork?*

"You just got off a plane three hours ago," he clarified. "Wouldn't you like to take the day to get settled in? We could start fresh first thing in the morning."

"What day of the week is this, Mr. Nolan?"

"Drew," he corrected her. "And I believe it's Monday, *Vic.*"

"Monday," she repeated. "Where I come from, Monday is the first day of the typical work week. And since it's only three o'clock, I'd say we have a good three hours left to our work day, wouldn't you?"

Raw irritation churned suddenly in acidic somersaults throughout Drew's stomach, and he followed the movement with a curt nod of his head.

"I'm ready when you are, Miss Townsend. The conference room is down that hall and to the left. The phone is in working order and I believe you'll find everything you need to get started in the supply closet inside. If you'll give me ten minutes, I'll join you with all the files you've requested."

Vic paused for a moment, just the slightest hint of something akin to bewilderment burning in her baby blues. He was stunned at the sudden urge to either turn her over his knee and spank her or jerk her into his arms and kiss her; neither option being anything he would have done, of course.

"Excellent," she finally responded, then spun around and headed down the hall.

Clicking his heels staunchly together in time with a military salute, Drew rigidly poked his tongue out at her departure.

"Ja, mein kommandant!" he whispered sarcastically.

Drew dissolved into a demeanor far more courteous as she turned back toward him.

"I beg your pardon?"

"Can I bring you anything to drink?" he asked politely. "Coffee? Snapple?"

"Nothing, thank you."

Once Vic had disappeared through the door to the conference room, Drew bowed slightly, rolling his arm before him like a sultan greeting royalty.

"I'm but here to serve, *Your Sourpuss.*"

Shaking his head and looking a bit like he'd just spit out the dregs of a bad batch of lemonade, Drew stomped over to the four-drawer file at the wall and dragged open the drawer.

"If I can interrupt your love life," he mimicked, squeezing up his face into a bitter contortion. *"Where I come from, Monday is the first day of our work week."*

He yanked several manila folders from the drawer and slapped them on the top of the steel cabinet so hard that the thing shook beneath the force.

"Where you come from, Monday is also the day that all the robots have their circuit breakers oiled and cleaned too!"

Snatching up the last of the files, he slammed the drawer shut with his fist before turning on his heels to come directly chest-to-face with the steely-cold stare of Victoria Townsend.

Chapter Three

She hadn't said a word in over thirty minutes, and Drew was sweating it out in a way that was reminiscent of the times he sat in his elementary school principal's office waiting for one of his parents to show up. Of course, Mr. Harrington would at least have cast him the occasional grimace over the top of the little square glasses perched at the tip of his nose; Vic hadn't even given him that much. She just sat there in the metal and upholstered chair at the other side of the conference table, immersed in the files he'd sheepishly handed her without a single word being exchanged between them.

Man, she'd make a good school principal, he thought. *Or a military interrogator.*

He could almost feel the heat of her lamp shining in his eyes.

"Snapple?" he finally asked, and the sound of his own voice seemed to shatter glass in the silence.

"Pardon?" Her blue eyes rose toward him, seeming to spear into him as they came to rest.

"Would you like something cold to drink? I have Snapple in the fridge."

"Oh, no, thanks. But you go ahead."

Drew popped to his feet and nudged open the small refrigerator in the corner. The cold brew of fruity iced tea felt exceptionally good as it made its way down his parched throat.

"Well, if you don't have any questions for me," he told her, "I have some calls to make."

"Actually," she said, and he froze there in the doorway, unaware at first that he'd stopped breathing, "I would like to talk to you. If you can give me a few minutes?"

"Sure," he tried to say casually, then slid into the seat of the backwards chair, straddling it and draping his arms over its back.

Vic pushed away from the table and relaxed slightly, sleekly crossing her legs and placing her folded hands gently into her lap. Those blue eyes of hers bore into him with all the intensity

23

of a science experiment he'd once conducted. It had to do with a ray of light and a magnifying glass, focused in on a sheet of paper in hopes of creating a flame. Drew found himself hoping he didn't spontaneously combust any time soon.

"I think I have a pretty good idea of what's going on here."

Drew stared back at her for a long moment. "Come again?"

"With your business," she said, and he released a sigh. "You've got a highly specialized service. You create romantic situations for the creatively-challenged. Some of it is ingenious, really. Take what you did for David Lutz, for instance."

Drew waited as she shuffled through the files before her and produced the green folder bearing Lutz's name.

"His intended bride . . ." she began, then searched the contents of the file for her name.

"Susan."

"Yes. Susan is somewhat of a nature enthusiast. And you arranged this whole parasailing adventure. And she saw the words *Marry Me, Susan* formed in the sand from up above."

"We used large stones, painted with orange neon," Drew interjected. He was proud of that one.

"And afterward there was a surprise moonlight cruise with her whole family aboard to celebrate," she added. "I'm curious, though. What if she'd refused his proposal?"

"That was never an option," Drew replied with a shrug. "They'd been together for three years. One of the most solid couples around."

Vic thought that over for a moment, then nodded. "I see."

She produced another folder from the pile and set it out between them.

"Carrie and George Kramer," she stated, tapping her fingernail at the center of their file. "She wanted to do something extraordinary to celebrate George's graduation from film school, and you arranged for a local theater to include an announcement slide in their pre-movie advertising."

Drew released a short chuckle at the memory. "We almost got burned on that one. At the last minute, old George started to consider seeing a romantic comedy instead of the action flick they'd discussed. Luckily, Carrie turned him around."

"These are clever and resourceful ideas," she told him. "Every one of them. I'd say you're quite adept at high concept. You just haven't concentrated on the bigger picture here."

"What do you mean?"

"Romantic Overtures is exclusive and specific. But you're catering to the average Joe on the street. Now there's nothing wrong with that, as long as you realize those Joes are not going to be the heart of your business. To keep that heart beating, you have to bring in the big ticket events. The big fat checkbooks and the high profile affairs. And you're not going to attract the big boys by advertising in the local freebie sheets or depending on word of mouth either."

Drew nodded thoughtfully. He had to admit, if only to himself, that he'd considered such notions more than a few times. But figuring out how best to act on it just hadn't yet ignited the dim light bulb hovering occasionally over his head.

"What do you think then?" he asked her seriously. "How do I draw in that kind of business?"

"Media attention comes to mind," she offered.

"Like taking out ads in bigger papers?"

"Well, Drew, that would be a start. But there's really no publicity like free publicity. Especially for a business in the financial condition of yours. I'd like to do some research of the area, examine our options. Then we'll discuss the possibility of creating a little hype over what you have to offer."

He considered her words, and then nodded. "Okay."

"Meanwhile," she said on a sigh, and then paused as she leaned back into the chair and stretched slightly, "don't you have a date?"

"Pardon?"

"I heard you on the phone before," she told him. "Something about meeting someone at sunset."

"Oh! No, that's not a date. I'm meeting a friend."

"Well, I'd say sunset is moving in on us," she remarked. "Hadn't you better get moving?"

"I guess I should, yes."

"I'll tidy up here and then give some thought to some dinner," she said, already straightening the files into a neat pile. "Where can I get some Chinese takeout?"

"There's a menu in the drawer of the reception desk," Drew replied. "Or I could bring you something back in an hour or so."

"No, you go ahead and meet your friend. I'll fend for myself. A little sesame chicken will go nicely with an evening on the internet."

A stifled grin rose to the surface in spite of his best efforts to suppress it, and Drew let out a little chuckle.

"What?"

"You just don't strike me as the chat room type," he admitted.

"The internet is a research tool, Mr. Nolan," she stated seriously. "I'll learn more about the demographics of this area of Florida in an hour on the internet than I could in two days of cruising the streets."

Of course. Business. I should have known.

"By the time the curtain goes down on your sunset, I'll be able to tell you our next move to put Romantic Overtures on the map of local commerce."

"Or," he began, shooting her a cock-eyed smile, "you could throw on some shorts and sandals and join us down at the beach. It's an awesome sight."

"You stick to your sunset," she said, almost returning his smile. "I'll stick to what I do best."

"You don't know what you're missing."

"Neither do you."

"Funny," Drew commented before getting to his feet and heading for the doorway.

"Oh, and Drew . . ."

He stopped, and then leaned one hip against the jamb.

"I'll make sure to oil and clean my circuit breakers while you're gone."

Heat rose instantly to his face, and Drew could feel it leaving a stain.

"I . . . I didn't mean . . ."

"Yes, you did," she said, and the smile that tenderly changed her face seemed to reach out and pinch the very center of his soul. "Believe me, I get a lot of that. But I'm really not such a horrible person underneath."

"N-no, I'm sure you're . . . very . . ."

"It's just that I'm here for a reason. To help turn your business around. And that's one thing I know how to do really well."

"And I appreciate it," he said softly. "I really do."

"All right then."

"Okay."

"Go see your sunset."

"Enjoy your sesame chicken."

"I will. Thanks."

Drew wondered, as he cut across the parking lot toward the spot where he and Penelope always met up, whether there really was the possibility of some softness at the core of Victoria Townsend. Beneath all that steel and muscle and menace pulled taut as a piano wire, was there a core of something light and carefree?

Nah, he decided. *She's just tired. She'll be back to her old self again in no time at all.*

"Louie!" he called as he jogged across the alley. "Lou!"

Louie appeared out of nowhere, barking out his excitement as he barreled past his master toward the beach that beckoned in the distance.

"Hey, wait for me!"

Vic climbed the stairs and examined the takeout menu as she let herself into the tiny apartment she must now call home. She dialed the bold-faced number at the top and gazed out the window as she waited.

She could make him out on the horizon. There was no mistaking Drew's form, even shadowed against the orange glow of the descending sun, long legs catapulting him across the sand, that ridiculous beast nipping at his heels.

"Yes, I'd like to place an order for delivery," she said softly into the receiver.

"Can you hold?"

"Yes."

Vic strained to get a clearer look at the profile that greeted Drew, shielding her eyes against the glare beyond. The two embraced for a moment, then locked arms, sauntering down the edge of the beach as if neither one of them had a care in the entire world outside of one another and the work of art forming watercolor streaks across a blue backdrop.

It pinched slightly to watch them, but Vic couldn't manage to look away. She wondered if she'd ever been so carefree with Richard, or with anyone else for that matter. There had been that vacation in Cabo San Lucas, she realized, grasping the memory with something akin to desperation, and then she deflated at the stark recollection that capped it. They had cut the trip short by three days when Vic had accessed the interoffice e-mail announcing the upcoming possibility of snagging the Reebok account. They had a good three months' notice, but Vic's mind had begun buzzing with activity that very day, and it was all she could do to sleep through the night before calling the airline and arranging a quick return to New York the following day.

"Your order?"

"Oh!" she exclaimed, wondering how long the line had been open without her noticing. "I'd like an order of sesame chicken, please. And some of your fried dumplings."

She couldn't make them out on the horizon any more, but she continued to try just the same as she depressed the button on the phone and dropped it to the table.

The lavender streaks across the sky gave way to a bolder purple bordered by splotches of pink and gold and deep blue. It truly was a magnificent sight, and Vic couldn't remember the last time she'd taken the time to observe a setting sun.

With a deep and weary sigh, she finally turned away. Slipping out of her shoes as she went, she padded over to the small dining table where she'd set up her laptop and dropped down in front of it.

"It sounds like she's pretty sharp anyway. Maybe you'll warm up to her."

"I did see a side to her earlier that was almost human."

Drew tossed a neon tennis ball down the beach, and Louie left a shower of sand and water in a trail behind him as he tore out after it.

"But I'm sure it was just a momentary lapse."

The last golden traces of the sun reflected its light in his friend's warm brown eyes, and her dark chocolate skin seemed to glisten at its touch. The hundred tiny corkscrew braids surrounding her oval face were held into place with a colorful scarf that matched the light cotton dress she wore, a rather shapeless shift that danced around her ankles with the kiss of the evening breeze. Penelope Cole was a beautiful African-American woman and, despite a good ten or twelve years in age between them, she was the best friend Drew had.

Looping her arm through his as they walked on, Penelope chuckled. "Well, you don't have to like her to learn from her, boy."

"It's a good thing too. Because I don't."

Louie trotted toward them, proudly displaying his prize. After he dropped the tennis ball at his master's feet, he began barking wildly with excitement.

"One more time," Drew warned him before pitching the ball down the beach for the eager dog, and then Louie was off again in hot pursuit.

"She seems to have some good ideas. If they translate into action, I'll learn to appreciate her."

"Well, dat's somethin' den," Penelope cracked in a forced Jamaican accent she hadn't really possessed in years.

"Do you want to come over for a drink?" Drew offered, but Penelope shook her head.

"My boy is due in tomorrow," she reminded him. "I have some seee-rious cookin' to do."

"I hope Terrence knows how fortunate he is to have a mother like you."

"When he lugs all that laundry home from the university, he knows," she replied on a burst of laughter. "And he'll just be down for a day or two, eating my food and lying around on my sofa, before he'll be more than ready to leave his mother far behind for another month or two."

"Ah, but you love every minute of it."

"I do, indeed."

"Louie!" Drew called, and the dog immediately headed back toward him, the tennis ball barely visible from its place between his clenched teeth, wedged behind a huge stick and some sort of wrapper he'd picked up along the way.

"That's the way, Louie," Penelope rewarded him as he reached them. "Always do your part to clean up our beaches."

Drew shook his head as he removed the debris from the mouth of his dog, and then he squatted down to rinse off the ball in what was left of the surf.

"Give my best to Terrence," Drew told her. "Maybe we can get together while he's here."

"If he can tear himself away from my sofa, I'll give you a ring."

"Sounds good."

Drew took Penelope into his arms and embraced her affectionately.

"Cook up a storm, woman."

"Will do," she answered, and planted a noisy kiss on his cheek in return.

"Let's go, Lou."

Drew took his time hiking through the sand, and then stamped it off his feet as he reached the pavement.

"Here," he said, bouncing the ball into Louie's open mouth. "Carry this home."

He turned to take one last look at the twilight sea, and then headed on his way beneath the flickering yellow streetlights that were just coming to life. When he rounded his own building, Louie's enthusiastic barking subsided into low, throaty growls, effectively announcing the presence of his out-of-town guest before he actually saw her.

"Oh, shut up," he heard Vic say just as he reached the top of the stairs, and she seemed embarrassed when she realized he had heard.

"His bark is much worse than his bite," he assured her.

"Well, I hope so," she returned, casting a wary glance at the snarling animal. "I don't think he likes me much."

"You'll grow on him," he commented as he passed.

Drew lingered at his front door and glimpsed back at Vic. She looked much softer than before, he couldn't quite place why until he noticed that her hair was piled upward, held off her slender china neck by several tiny clips. Soft wisps had escaped and curled seductively around her face, which was turned up into the night sky. Leaning casually over the iron rail with her eyes gently closed, she looked to Drew as if she were conjuring up dreams of some distant comfort.

"G'night," he offered as he turned the knob.

"Oh," she returned on a sigh, then opened her eyes and glanced at him, almost sweetly. "Good night."

He half expected a last-minute command, something about resuming their business bright and early in the morning, and he paused just inside the apartment in anticipation. But the command didn't follow, and he softly closed the door behind him.

Chapter Four

"What was that? Was that the click of a lighter?"

Vic scowled at the phone as she drew in her first lungful of smoke from the newly-lit cigarette between her fingers.

"What are you?" she asked Krissy with a groan. "The cigarette gestapo?"

"Vic, for pity's sake. You've got to at least try to quit. You know what the doctor said."

"Have I fired you yet today?"

Krissy's immediate giggle brought a chuckle out of Vic.

"Not yet. But it's early, so you still have time. Pace yourself."

"You're going to fax me the stats the minute you get them, right?"

"You'll have them before noon."

"Thank you," she sang in what had become the routine manner of dismissing her assistant.

"Welcome," Krissy returned, as always.

Vic placed the receiver into its cradle and took another drag from her cigarette.

Nothing that feels so good should be so bad for you, she thought, then held up the cigarette and stared at it for a moment.

With all the determination she could muster, she padded across the floor toward the ashtray on the kitchen counter. She took one last drag before stamping out the fire and setting the unsmoked remnant next to several others.

"Don't smoke. Take your meds. Eat right. Learn to relax," she recited bitterly. "What's next? Take up jogging?"

She stepped over to the sink and drained filtered water from the jug on the windowsill into a glass before doling out the regimen of morning pills and swallowing them down.

"Thirty-three years old, and this is the life I'm resigned to."

Vic set the glass down on the counter with a clank, and then headed off toward the bedroom to get dressed. She leafed through the clothes hanging in the closet in an effort to find something that wouldn't leave her miserable in the ungodly

Florida heat, and finally settled on one of the few lightweight fabrics she owned. She slipped into a short-sleeved white tee shirt, and then slid the blue cotton jumper over her head. It was an outfit normally reserved for Sunday morning outings for bagels and coffee and *The New York Times.* As she inspected the knee-length hemline in the mirror, she sadly acknowledged the paste-white flesh of her legs.

Oh, Mr. Suntan should really get a laugh out of this.

Vic sat down on the edge of the bed and laced up the white Keds she'd almost forgotten she owned until she'd begun packing for this adventure, then wiggled her toes inside of them. Her feet hadn't donned anything so comfortable besides bedroom slippers in at least a year's time. Wouldn't her stepfather be proud to see what she'd finally been reduced to?

"Okay! What do you say we get down to business!" she announced as she burst through the office door a few minutes later.

Her first greeting was the immediate and monotonous drone of growls and barks she had nearly been able to forget.

"Hey," she called out, her eyes never leaving the dog for an instant. "Hey! Can you call off the border police here?"

"Louie! Back off!"

Vic raised her eyes reluctantly to find a stranger standing before her, and was relieved to discover that the dog responded obediently, wagging his tail wildly as he trotted around the girl, and then planting himself at her side.

"You must be Vic," she said with a toothy grin.

"Yes," she replied, giving Louie a quick glance before walking inside and shutting the door behind her.

"I'm Tiffany."

This was not the persona Vic had summoned up at the original mention of the girl's name. *Tiffany* conjured up visions of a college cheerleader, honey-haired and blue-eyed, all bounce and old money. Not a stark-white platinum blonde with no more than an inch of hair sticking straight up on her head, a tattooed flock of butterflies encircling her upper arm, and a tiny gold nose ring!

"You're . . . Tiffany?"

"Uh-huh," the girl grinned at her. "I used to live upstairs where you are now. I help Drew out around the office sometimes."

"Yes. He mentioned you."

"Oh, good. I'm running out for a smoothie. Would you like one?"

"A smoothie?"

"Fruit? Ice? You drink it?"

"Oh."

"Would you like one?"

"N-no, thank you."

"Okay. Well, I'll be back in a few minutes."

Vic watched out the window as the girl straddled some sort of small neon motorcycle and sped off down the street.

That's Tiffany?

Louie's low growl brought her back into the moment, and she carefully inched her way past him, then hurried down the hall toward the conference room.

Drew looked to her like something out of one of those trendy ads for what passed for casual clothing these days. Baggy tan shorts were topped off by a black short-sleeved shirt that wasn't tucked in at the waist, and his feet were slipped casually into a pair of worn black Birkenstocks with double buckles. He was at least clean-shaven today, but his hair was somewhat mussed and Vic wondered if he'd even bothered to run a comb through it that morning.

A spell seemed to be broken when he did run a hand through his sandy mane of hair, and Vic blinked hard and straightened before he looked up.

"Good morning," she said, then walked into the room as if she'd just arrived.

"Morning," he replied with a smile, and he leaned back into his chair and folded both hands behind his head as he seemed to inspect her with maddening severity. His scrutiny made her uncomfortable, and Vic glared back at him for a moment.

"Well, look at you."

"What does that mean?" she asked curtly, then planted herself in the chair opposite him at the table.

"Why, you're almost casual this morning," he observed. "You wear it well."

"I'm glad you approve. Now, what are you working on?"

Drew's cockeyed grin remained in place as he leaned forward and tapped the paperwork before him.

"Tiffany's wedding."

"She's . . . engaged?" Vic couldn't help but wonder what the fiancé must look like!

"Walter Weems," he stated, then let out a sigh. "And he's in for quite a surprise."

Walter Weems?

It sounded like the name of a bank manager or a history teacher! No Walter-like individual Vic had ever known would have found himself involved with the likes of the girl she had just met.

"Tiff is planning a wedding that will straighten the starch in Walter's tie," he said with a slight chuckle.

"The girl I just met in the office," Vic stated, just to clarify, "she's marrying a tie-donning fellow named Walter?"

"I know," Drew replied as he nodded at her. "Love builds all sorts of bridges."

"Apparently," she conceded. "Can I see what you're planning?"

"Everything in the wedding will be W-themed," he told her, spinning the yellow pad in front of him across the table toward her.

"W?"

"Despite what you might guess from her appearance," he seemed to be chastising her without cause, "Tiffany is a very romantic soul."

"Really." It was more of a statement of consideration than a question of the fact.

"I'll let her explain it to you when she gets back," he seemed to decide on the spot. "But everything in the wedding will be based on W."

"As in *Walter Weems.*"

"Correct. The wedding will be held out on the beach, and the minister performing the ceremony is Reverend Garrison Wales. The chairs for the guests will be arranged in the pattern of a W."

"That will make the walk down the aisle a little . . . uh . . . jagged, won't it?"

Drew rose to his feet and leaned across the table toward her, and she watched him warily as he did. Finally, he reached out and turned over a page on the yellow pad, and she resisted the urge to release the sigh of relief that built instantly in her lungs. Tapping his finger on the pad, he pointed out a sketch centered around the shape of a large W.

"She'll walk straight up the middle, right here," he told her, tracing the path along the makeshift map, then dabbing several times at the very center of the W with his fingertip. "The minister will be standing right here."

"Weverend Wales," Vic clarified.

A slight puff of amusement punctuated Drew's retreat back across the table and down to the chair behind him.

"There will be parchment programs—"

"White, no doubt."

"—in the shape of the letter W."

"Of course."

"Her bouquet—"

"Willow branches?"

"Wisteria."

"Ah. Tell me she's not planning to march down the aisle to *Wipeout.*"

Drew shook his head as if he were one part amused and two parts simply disgusted with her.

"Are you making fun of me, Vic?"

A rush of heat moved through her, and she looked up to find Tiffany standing in the doorway, two large paper cups in her hands, and Louie standing at her feet, panting softly.

He picks now to stop barking out an announcement for everything that moves?

"I'm sorry," she offered sincerely. "I've just never heard of this kind of theme for a wedding."

"Does she have to work on this one, Drew?"

"No," he replied, gathering the paperwork on the table and placing it into the accordion file at his side. "She doesn't. You'll have to excuse our guest, Tiff. She's just getting acclimated, and no one's introduced her to the notion of social graces yet."

With that, Drew rose from the chair and marched out, placing an arm around Tiffany's shoulder and guiding her along with him.

"Wait a minute," Vic called out, but the flap of two sets of sandals against barefoot heels let her know that they weren't considering a return. "I'm . . . I'm sorry . . ." But she knew the slight giggle that followed didn't exactly represent sincerity.

Louie lingered in the doorway for a moment, emitting a low and unfriendly growl before trotting off to join them in their departure. A moment later, the front door thudded shut, and Vic leaned back into the chair and groaned.

"Oh . . . phooey."

Vic's eyes were burning when she finally snapped shut her laptop. The clock read 7:18 p.m., and the tug in her stomach reminded her that she hadn't eaten anything for most of the day.

She'd photocopied the delivery menus she'd found in the office and brought them up to the apartment, so she shuffled through them in search of something that struck her fancy. She landed on a pizza place, and tried to steer the meal halfway near healthy by ordering a salad to go along with it.

Plucking a cigarette out of the pack on the counter, she poked it into her mouth and grabbed for a light. Then, with the irritating voice of her assistant cackling in her ears, she slid the thing back into the pack and pushed it across the tile.

"There. Happy, Krissy?"

A gentle rap drew her across the living room, and the familiar cacophony of barks and growls as she unlatched the chain announced the visitor before she could open the door.

"Louie! Can it!"

Drew stood before her, a large cardboard box filling both of his extended arms.

"This came for you this afternoon."

"Oh, thanks," she said, opening the door to let him in. "Can you put it down on the table?"

He walked in without a word, and Louie followed as if he owned the place.

"I don't remember inviting you," she said to the dog, but both master and faithful beast ignored the comment.

"Okay," Drew stated when he'd set down the box. "Well, I'll see you later then."

"Wait," she blurted suddenly, and then let out a sigh. "Wait a minute, will you?"

He sure wasn't going to make this painless; she could see that by his demeanor. He just stood there rigidly, as if impatiently waiting for some insignificant slice of information that he was already sure would mean nothing.

"Look," she began. "I just ordered a pizza. Do you want to stay and share it with me? Save me and my cholesterol count from ourselves."

"No, thanks." And with that, he was in motion, heading for the door.

"Wait," she repeated, and he paused a moment before turning around to face her. "Look, I'm really sorry about this morning."

"You're telling the wrong person, Miss Townsend."

"I know. I do. And I'm going to apologize to Tiffany too. It was insensitive of me to mock her wedding plans. That was just . . . so . . . wrong. And I'm very sorry."

His silence seemed to scream at her, and his blue-green eyes pierced her to her very core.

"You're not going to make this easy on me, are you?" she asked him finally, and an uneasy chuckle followed involuntarily.

"Should I?"

"Well," she began, and then fell silent for a moment. "I'd appreciate it if you would. You know. Just a little."

He shot her a somewhat bitter attempt at a smile. "I'm sure you would."

"Come on. I said I was sorry. Can't we try and be friends again?"

"Friends?" he repeated softly.

"Well, we have to work together. We may as well be civil. And I really am sorry. My behavior was . . . was . . ."

"Insensitive?"

"Yes."

"Ill-mannered."

"Okay. Yes."

"Somewhat cruel and—"

"Okay!" she stopped him, and then awkwardly tried to smile. "Have you been reading the thesaurus again?"

"Miss Townsend, look—"

"Vic. Come on. Don't call me Miss Townsend. It makes me feel like I'm the IRS auditor."

"If you don't want to feel like that, stop acting like it," he pointed out. "You are not the Queen Bee, and we your subservient drones. I'm trying to build a business here, and I was hoping you would help me do that. But it doesn't mean I now work for you. This is not a military recognizance mission, and we're not staging a corporate coup. You're here to consult. Are we clear?"

"Yes."

Vic forced back any additional comment, then clamped shut her lips for a long moment, folding them into her mouth and securing them with her teeth, just to ensure her own silence.

"Enjoy your pizza," Drew said as he turned back toward the door.

Any further invitation to share her dinner was buried along with the myriad smart-mouthed responses that wanted to plunge through the surface of her resolve.

"Thanks, I will."

His departure was quick, and Vic released the death grip on her lips, contorting them in an effort to stretch them back into shape.

"If you ask me, you could stand a bit of a coup around here," she muttered at the closed door, and then padded off into the kitchen.

Vic picked up the cigarette she'd tossed to the counter and inspected it almost lovingly. With a groan, she slipped it into the pocket of her jumper and returned to the living room.

After a moment of aimless wandering, she landed on the box Drew had deposited on the table in front of the sofa.

"Let's see what you've sent me, Krissy," she said, tearing into the cardboard box.

Tucked neatly into it were several magazines with colorful post-it notes marking certain pages. Vic folded down to the sofa as she leafed through them.

A copy of *O Magazine* was on top, and the article flagged was called "Remembering Your Spirit." She tossed it beside her on the couch and moved on to the next one. Several copies of *Cosmopolitan* offered two articles on the importance of keeping physically fit and a quiz entitled, "Are You Married To Your Job?" Vic released a sigh and tossed them aside as well.

She reached into the box and produced a can of unsalted, raw almonds bearing a white hand-written label. "Salt is bad for high blood pressure. Try these."

Several jars of vitamin supplements followed, and then a small array of romance novels, the top one displaying a label marked: "In case you've forgotten how." Five packs of chewing gum succeeded an assortment of soothing caffeine-free teabags and a box containing a step-by-step program and the nicotine patch.

At the very bottom, she discovered a large bar of chocolate, and Vic pulled it from the box excitedly and tore open the wrapper. Popping a chunk of the treat into her mouth, she closed her eyes and sighed with delight before tearing open a company envelope bearing her name. She slipped out the hand-written note inside.

Don't make me come down there and show you how it's done, Boss. Take care of yourself. Stop that awful smoking, and get some sunshine and rest. I'm worried about you. Love, Krissy.

Vic rolled her eyes slightly and broke off another piece of chocolate before continuing on to the postscript.

P.S. The chocolate is for emergency use only. Don't just eat it and toss the rest of your care package away.

A pang of guilty irritation cut a laser path through her chest, and she gingerly folded the aluminum packaging around what was left of the chocolate bar and set it on the table. Vic rose from the couch and meandered over to the large window and stared out toward the surf in the distant night, fondling the cigarette buried in her pocket.

Louie announced the arrival of the pizza delivery guy, and Vic crossed to the table, producing some cash from her wallet before heading toward the door. When she opened it, the uniformed boy was just reaching the top of the stairs, the incited dog in close pursuit.

"Is he safe?" the kid asked her cautiously, glancing back at Louie who was alternating between snarls and barks.

"I don't really know," she replied casually, handing over the twenty-dollar bill and ignoring the expression of alarm on the boy's face. "Keep the change."

Carefully negotiating the space between Louie and the building wall, the poor boy took the stairs two at a time and hightailed it back to his car. The dog didn't follow, and Vic stared at him curiously.

"Are you safe?" she asked him, and Louie responded by growling softly at first, and then lowering his ears and panting at her with something that resembled a queer smile.

Vic shrugged before stepping inside the apartment, the food delivery boxes balanced on her arm.

"Go play menacing somewhere else," she told Louie. "I'm not in the mood." And she was rather surprised when he turned on his heels and retreated without further comment.

She looked on for a moment as he trotted happily down the landing toward the apartment next door.

"Crazy dog," she mumbled, and then headed inside to inspect her dinner.

Chapter Five

Vic plugged the cable into the printer, and then tapped the command button on her laptop at the precise moment that the office door opened and Tiffany stepped inside.

"Good, you're here," she said with a grin, but Tiffany didn't crack a smile.

"I told you on the phone that I'd come," the girl replied seriously. "Now, what's this all about?"

"Yes," Drew added suspiciously as he appeared in the hall. "What's going on?"

"I called and asked Tiffany if she would meet me," Vic explained, then snatched the page from the printer and looked it over. Suppressing the smile on her face, she looked Tiffany in the eye. "I wanted to apologize to you for my behavior the other day."

She paused for a moment, giving the girl an opportunity to interject something, anything, but the only thing that greeted her was a curious stare.

"It was completely unprofessional," Vic continued. "The only excuse I have to offer is that the whole concept of Drew's business itself is so foreign to me. I've spent my entire career dealing with running shoes and clothing lines and cat food. Pretty unromantic stuff."

Tiffany's shrug was slight, but detectable. Vic discerned it as a signal that she was softening, and wasted no time in capitalizing on the faint progress.

"I hope you'll accept my apology," she said sincerely.

"Well," the girl said, mellowing. "Okay."

"Great!" Vic exclaimed, and then extended a handshake which Tiffany accepted. "And in honor of that, I have something to show you."

Tiffany glanced at Drew before taking the sheet of paper Vic offered, and he moved in closer, peering over Tiffany's shoulder as she inspected it.

"What is this?" she asked.

"I have an associate in New York," she explained, "that does some work for our company every now and then. Maybe you saw one of the pieces on television about the crystal pins that were designed for Cutting Edge Computers in conjunction with the millennium celebration?"

" 'The bridge to the future,' " Tiffany recited. "They were little Golden Gate Bridges."

"Well, yes. They were modeled after that bridge."

"That was you?"

"It was my concept, yes."

Tiffany turned toward Drew. "They ended up a collector's item," she told him excitedly. "And then there were T-shirts and billboards. Stony Gray wore one when he accepted his Best New Artist Grammy."

"Really," he stated with a nod, and when he raised his eyes to meet Vic's, a slight current of electricity made its way all the way through her.

"Well, anyway," she swallowed, "last night, I called Peter Engle, the gentleman who designed those pins for us and told him about you."

"About me?"

"Yes, about your whole W-themed idea. And I asked him if he could kick around some ideas for a wedding cake ornament for you."

"Are you joking?"

"No. And this is what he faxed me this morning!"

Tiffany and Drew simultaneously dropped their attention back to the sheet of paper before them.

"It would be formed out of crystal hearts," she explained, running her finger along the shape of the W. "And if you look closely, you can see that it's actually two hands clasped together."

Tiffany raised her eyes to Vic again, and then blinked dramatically.

"You don't like it?" Vic asked, harboring her disappointment just below the surface.

"No, no," Tiffany replied. "It's beautiful. But . . . well . . . this is going to be really expensive, and . . ."

"Oh! No," Vic reassured her. "Peter sort of owes me a favor, and he's going to do this for us, *gratis.*"

Tiffany blinked again.

"For free," she expounded, and the girl released a deep sigh.

"Why would he do that?" she asked.

"Well, mainly because I asked him to," she boasted, ever so slightly.

"I don't get it," Tiffany observed, then looked back to Drew once more before returning her full attention to Vic. "Why would *you* do that?"

"Tiffany, I felt terrible about what happened the other day. And I got to thinking about your wedding idea, and I realized it's actually quite high concept. It would be just the sort of thing that would get Romantic Overtures some great publicity. Not just on a local level, but nationally."

"Wait a minute," Drew interrupted, and he made a slashing motion across his neck as if he were the director of this film and had decided to call a cut. "You haven't even discussed this with me."

"Well, that's what I'm doing right now," she replied. "We could generate some real attention here."

"You're not going to use Tiffany's wedding as a publicity ploy to advance my business."

"Why not? You said yourself that Tiffany and Walter are as ill-suited as they could be—"

"You said what?" Tiffany grimaced.

"I never said ill-suited," he insisted.

"—and that true love builds unexpected bridges between people like them," Vic continued without pause.

"You said that?" The girl softened. "That's sort of sweet."

"And from your reference about building bridges, I jumped over to Peter's bridge pins—"

"That was quite a leap," he grumbled.

"—and then there I was," she explained animatedly. "Building bridges, Peter's pins, Tiffany's wedding, the wedding cake, and *bam!*"

"She's really good at this publicity stuff," Tiffany observed seriously, and Drew cast her a glare that might have cut glass. "Well, she is."

"And what better demonstration of this business' creativity and its involvement in the course of true romance than its sponsorship of a Walter-centered, W-themed wedding!" Vic summarized enthusiastically.

"Wow," Tiffany said on a sigh. "I'm exhausted just listening."

"A different reaction comes to my mind," Drew snarled.

"Come on, Drew, it's a great idea, and you know it!" Vic pushed. "As long as you wouldn't mind, Tiffany. I mean, a wedding is a private and intimate event in a young woman's life."

"Precisely!" he exclaimed.

"And if you would feel invaded or infringed upon in any way, of course, we wouldn't do it." *Please, don't tell me not to do it!* "But the kind of exposure I think I can drum up over this for Romantic Overtures," she continued without pause, "would benefit you and Walter as well. Costs would probably be cut drastically if we negotiated it right. I understand you'll want to discuss the whole thing with Walter first."

"No!" Tiffany squealed. "The whole thing is supposed to be a surprise for him."

"A surprise wedding?" Vic cried. This was almost too good to be true! "That's even better."

"I wanted to do the whole thing as a sort of gift to him," the girl explained. "He just gave me a budget and helped me set the date. The rest of it is completely my baby."

"You," Vic hooted, placing both of her hands on either side of Tiffany's face, "are a public relations dream!"

"You really think so?"

"Hello?" Drew interjected provisionally. "Remember me? I own this business?"

"Your wedding will be as memorable as you've dreamed it would be," Vic told Tiffany without notice. "And Walter will be knocked right off his—Ooooh! And you know what? Have you chosen your dress yet?"

"Well, I've narrowed it down to three options," she replied. "I'm not all that excited about any of them, really."

"I know this great up-and-coming designer in Greenwich. She's very good, and she's very hungry. If I can produce enough interest, we might be able to persuade her to help out there."

"A one-of-a-kind dress? Just for me?"

"I can't promise anything until I make some calls," she warned. "But I've got a very good feeling about this."

"That makes one of us," Drew faintly tossed in.

"Oh, thank you, Vic!" Tiffany cried, then threw her arms around Vic's neck and hugged her so tightly that she had to struggle to catch her breath. "If I didn't have a class to run to this afternoon, I swear I'd enlist as your slave!"

"Go to your class," she said with a giggle. "But call me at the end of the week, and I'll let you know what kind of progress I'm making."

"I will, I promise!"

Vic watched her bounce out the door, and her heart soared over the girl's enthusiasm. When she'd come up with the initial idea and then called Tiffany to come over, she'd expected some sort of argument, at the very least. But it was apparent to her that a brilliant concept was recognizable to lay people as well as media experts, and the realization deepened her fervor to bring the idea to life.

"This is going to be so great for your business, Drew!"

When he didn't respond, Vic turned quickly to face him. Rather than excitement or joy, or even the faintest recognition of an exceptional idea, she was met instead with the intense and possibly angry stare of a man on the verge of implosion.

"Are you out of your mind?"

The words slipped out before he'd been able to adjust the inner treble of his pitch.

"What do you mean?"

What do I mean? What do I MEAN?

"Are you socially impaired in some way?" he asked her seriously. "Didn't your rich stepdaddy think to send you to some sort of finishing school or something before unleashing you on the general public?"

"Drew, what's wrong?" Vic asked, all wide-eyed and infuriatingly ignorant. "I thought this was what you wanted."

"You never gave one single thought to what I wanted, Townsend! Let's just cut to the chase here. How dare you use that girl's wedding as a tool to steamroll right over me just for the sake of—"

"I'm not using her, Drew."

"You didn't want to come here in the first place. And the fact that you were sent here anyway—probably the first time in your whole miserable life that you didn't get exactly what you wanted, I might add— sent you completely over the edge. That's it, isn't it? You wanted revenge, and this is your way of getting it."

"Revenge?"

"Revenge!" he seethed. "And you're not going to stop until I call Trenton and beg him, plead with him, to reel you back in, are you? Well, that's what you want, honey, that's what you've got! I surrender. You've paid me back in full for ever having the audacity to reach out and ask for help."

"Drew, please, I thought I was doing something good. I thought . . ."

"You thought you'd found the only way to get what you really wanted. To be rid of me and Florida . . . and Louie . . . and . . . and this horrible slum of a setback in your life. And you know what? You were right. You found the way back home. I'll have your flight to New York arranged first thing in the morning."

"No, Drew. That's not—"

"Just don't say anything else. I've never been so sorry to have met anyone in my life. Now stop messing around with things you can't possibly understand and get out of my office."

"You're throwing me out?"

Her wide blue eyes and injured face were not going to work on him!

"That's what I'm doing, honey. Now, go pack your bags."

They both just stood there for a long moment, frozen in time, staring at one another in some sort of stunned horror. Drew might have thought the deep bass pounding in his ears could have been coming from the bar down the street if it hadn't been keeping perfect time with the thud against his chest.

"I'm sorry," she said hoarsely, and then one single tear cascaded down the slope of her face.

Drew's senses reeled as if on some sort of inner tilt-a-whirl, but before he could properly guage his response, she turned away from him and walked straight out the door.

"Look, Trenton, there's nothing I can do about it now. If he doesn't want my help, there's really no reason for me to remain in Florida."

"Just stay put," Trenton replied, and Vic marveled at her stepfather's ability to present a three-word statement in the unmistakable form of a supreme high command. "I'll talk to him and get back with you later this afternoon."

You do that, Vic thought as she replaced the telephone to its cradle. *Meanwhile, I'll keep on packing.*

Returning to the bedroom, she set about the task already at hand, and folded the next item of clothing at the top of the pile set out on the bed, tucking it neatly into the open suitcase.

She hadn't heard a peep out of Drew Nolan in the seventeen hours or so since he'd issued his eviction, but she knew enough about people to know that he hadn't been fooling around. The bitter taste at the back of her throat reminded her how disappointed Tiffany was going to be when she heard the news. And if Vic were truly honest with herself, which she had no desire to be at just that moment, she would have had to admit that she was a little disappointed herself.

It had taken nearly a week to get into the swing of things in Florida, but the fresh charge of the W-themed wedding concept had brought with it an unexpected enthusiasm about Florida in general. Vic had arrived at the Tampa International Airport empty-hearted, no tangible hope of being able to do anything extraordinary for a failing business such as Romantic Overtures and no real driving force to try. But Tiffany's wedding had spurred on a whole new resolve, and the eager response she'd received from Peter Engle had only served to add fuel to a fire that had already begun to rage within her.

Leave it to Andrew Nolan to douse the nearest inferno with his own brand of narrow thinking, she decided, tossing the final folded blouse to the top of the case and tipping it loosely shut.

Vic wondered what it was about men like Drew, so limited in their ability to see a picture broader than the meager angle in their immediate range, so reluctant to imagine a slightly more liberal scope. She'd known people like him in her life, of course, but she could never manage to connect with them in any meaningful way because of these self-imposed limitations they wielded around as freely as a fly swatter on a summer evening.

And yet Vic had sensed something forming between herself and Drew over the days prior to this setback. She'd only just begun to reconsider him, and had seen that Andrew Nolan was brimming with potential and limitless possibilities for success, and yet he had chosen in those final hours to wear it like an uncomfortable borrowed coat, shrinking back from it at the last in a disappointing display of what Vic could only view as pure cowardice.

A favorite quote from her college days suddenly came to mind, and she saddened at the memory. William Faulkner had written that success was a quality that was feminine and very much like a woman. "If you cringe before her," he had observed, "she will override you." And success had indeed driven straight over Drew Nolan on the previous day, leaving him flat and lifeless in her mind once again.

She made her way out to the kitchen to sort through the limited personal effects, such as medications and snacks. Noticing that the trash was brimming toward the top, she tugged at the drawstring and pulled the bag from the can. She thought for a moment that she might set it outside the door, and then reconsidered when she noticed Louie lounging a few feet down the landing in front of his master's door.

Vic trotted down the concrete stairs and deposited the bag in the bin at the side of the building, then climbed back up them to the top and stopped in anticipation. But Louie didn't greet her with his usual peal of warning, and she cocked her head in wonder as their eyes met.

"What's the matter, boy? Cat got your tongue?"

The reminder seemed to be just what he needed, and the dog set about his usual alarm of distinct snarls and barks.

"Woo, woo, woo," he seemed to be proclaiming, and Vic shook her head in his general direction.

"That's more like it," she said with a chuckle, careful to avoid his direct path on the trek back toward her door.

"C'mon, Lou, give it a rest."

When Drew appeared at the top of the stairs behind her, Vic met his gaze for only an instant before averting her eyes and lowering her head.

Chapter Six

"I'm glad you're here," Drew said softly, as Vic paused in the doorway and glanced back toward him.

Noticing the folded piece of paper in his hand, she asked, "Is that my travel itinerary?"

"Oh, no," he replied, and he gave the crease a quick renewal. "Can I talk to you a minute?"

"Come on in."

Vic walked back into the apartment, leaving the gaping door as the only further invitation. She was already seated in the armchair by the window when Drew finally made his way inside, Louie close at his heels.

"I've been speaking to Trent," he announced as he shut the door and stood rigidly in front of it.

"I can only imagine," she commented softly.

"And, well, he reminded me of something that I guess I already knew."

That I'm a pain in the butt? Vic wondered.

"You are very good at what you do."

Vic raised her eyes and focused intently on him.

"And I did come to your company asking for help," he added, and then perched gently on the arm of the couch.

"Yes," she acknowledged, "you did."

"This company is very important to me right now," Drew expounded.

"Trenton explained that to me when he asked me to come down here," Vic told him. "He told me to do whatever I could to bring it around."

"Look, I'm sure you meant well with Tiffany," he said seriously, "and there might even be something to what you proposed. But I guess I had an entirely different idea of what you'd be doing here."

"Why don't you tell me what you were expecting."

Drew propped the paper he'd been holding on the arm of the couch behind him, and then ran both hands through his disheveled hair before standing up and walking over to the front of the sofa. He appeared to fold completely in half as he sat down directly across from her, propping his elbows on both knees and folding his hands seriously before leaning forward.

"Instead of that," he suggested, "let's hear what you had in mind."

Vic was stunned. No, more than stunned, she was rendered speechless. And that had almost never happened to her before!

"I'm serious," he added cautiously. "I want to hear what you think might improve upon what I've got going here. I'd like the chance to consider your advice."

"Well," she began, leaning back into the chair and crossing one leg over the other. She exhaled a short burst of air that propelled her bangs upward before allowing them to fall back across her brows. "I think there is a niche out there that hasn't yet been filled by what Romantic Overtures might have to offer."

"Okay."

"First, I believe the company is too branched out, scattered in its approach."

"Can you explain that?" he asked calmly, if somewhat reservedly as well.

"Try thinking of your business in terms of a tree, rather than a full garden. Right now, you've got roses growing on this end, and tulips over there, and violets around the edges. Now, these are all beautiful flowers, but they require very diverse forms of specific care. So you're scattered. If you cultivate your business like a tree instead, with various branches off the same foundational root, I think you can make it into something strong; something that thrives."

Drew narrowed his eyes, the green of them glistening with intensity, and Vic received a form of unspoken, yet very vivid, encouragement from the look of them.

"I've done some interesting research," she told him as she rose from the chair. Drew silently followed her motion toward the dining room table, still littered with the controlled mess of paperwork surrounding her laptop. "There are a lot of companies out there that provide services such as wedding consultation, or travel planning for the honeymoon. But there are very few, and specifically none in the entire southeast region, that provide ongoing focus all the way from the proposal through the honeymoon."

"So you're saying you think I should give up the Harriet Peppersons and concentrate on the Tiffany and Walters," he surmised as he flipped one of the chairs around and straddled it backwards. "It seems to me that giving up business in the hand results in a loss of revenue, not an increase."

"But with that kind of streamlined tapering, you now know precisely what market you're reaching out to, and you are able to step into a niche that no other service in the area provides."

After a few minutes of silent and scrupulous consideration, Drew's gaze focused in on Vic, and he smiled.

"Go on."

Laying out her plan in minute detail consumed the better part of two hours, but Vic was encouraged by Drew's ability to grasp each procedural segment and apply it to his corporate future with practicality and understanding. Although he obviously battled simultaneously with uncertainty and trepidation, she was heartened by his willingness to hear her out and ask questions as they occurred to him.

"It's not really that big of a change in the overall mission statement of what you've already got in place," she explained in summary. "But I think the potential is there to grow in a way that you might not have been able to without the new focus."

Drew released a sigh laden with anxious excitement, and it bounced out at the end with a chuckle of concern.

"You could even find yourself going national, if things proceed the way I think that they can," Vic added as a means of encouragement. "I can't guarantee you success, of course. No one could do that. But I'm offering you what I believe is my best advice for your business, and you can make a decision from there."

Drew's eyes narrowed again, and the vehemence of his unspoken words compelled her to respond.

"What?"

"I'm just wondering," he replied at last. "Why couldn't we

have had this discussion prior to you jumping in with Tiffany and just laying it on me the way you did?"

Vic's eyes widened, and she tried to cast him a smile.

"You remember what you said about me not having social graces?" she asked timidly, and he nodded slightly. "I suppose, in a way, you were right."

Drew's laughter was restrained, but honest.

"My assistant tells me all the time," she admitted, "that I'm ninety-five percent corporate, and only about five percent human. I think it's something I'm going to start working on."

Drew looked away thoughtfully for a moment, and then returned her smile. And it was a smile filled with genuine warmth that she felt as physically as if it had been a well-stoked ember, burning its way into her flesh.

"Well, if you'll do that, how about if I try to work in the other direction and meet you in the middle," he offered, and Vic was drawn to it with all of the enchantment and fascination of a fairy tale princess to a knight on his steed.

"Mr. Nolan," she said with a grin, extending her hand toward him, "you've got yourself a deal."

The sun hovered for a while before continuing its descent toward the horizon, and Drew was glad for the extra time. There was nothing like these occasional moments at the beach with Penelope to help him put his days into better perspective.

"I'm sorry I'm late," Penelope declared as she tromped across the sand toward him. "Teaching these summer classes is a bear."

"I can relate."

"Oh no," she said, reaching around his neck with a welcoming embrace, and then planting a peck of a kiss on his waiting cheek. "What's she done now?"

"Actually—" He beamed, and Penelope broke into unabashed laughter before he ever got the words out.

"You've made friends with the pit bull then!"

"Let's just say she's exposed her soft underbelly, and I'm feeling a little more secure."

"That's a good thing then."

"I believe it is."

Penelope slipped out of her shoes, and then slipped her arm through Drew's before leading him down the beach. On their way, he recounted the story, from Tiffany's original visit on through to his meeting with Vic in her apartment, experiencing a surge of unexpected excitement at the prospect of pursuing her many concepts for development.

"The girl's got a good business head on those shoulders of hers," Penelope observed. "She might be just the thing to carry you through."

"Well, she's certainly overflowing with ideas," he acknowledged. "She's been doing this a long time, with a great deal of success. I don't see any harm in allowing her to teach me a thing or two."

"There's never harm in learning."

The twosome trudged on in silence for a while, their arms loosely interlocked. They gazed out at the setting sun with contented faces while Louie poled along behind them. Drew flattened the palm of his hand and rested it gently over Penelope's.

"She makes you happy then," she stated softly.

"Her business sense makes me ecstatic."

"I don't mean just in business. I'm talking about a more personal level. There's quite a change in you today."

"It's just relief," he replied.

"No, it's not. It's much more than that. Tell me what you're feeling."

"What are you talking about?" Drew objected, maybe just a tad too strenuously. "My business may just survive, and you know what that means to me in the broader scope. It leaves me feeling relieved."

"I'm not inquiring about what you're feeling in here," she said, tapping two fingers to the hollow point of his temple. "I want to know what you're feeling in here," and she thumped her fist lightly against the center of his chest.

"Well, right now I'm feeling pain where my best friend punched me," he teased, tugging at her arm to continue their journey along the shore.

"All right then," Penelope finally surrendered. "I'll wait. You'll be wanting to talk about it sooner or later."

"Talk about what?" Drew teased, shaking his lowered head. "You're a crazy old woman, do you know that?"

"Who you callin' old, boy!"

Vic stood up from the table and vigorously stretched until various muscles throughout her body yanked her back. It had been a long afternoon of inspecting the websites of wedding planners and travel agencies, florists and designers. Taking inspiration from various sources, she'd compiled at least ten pages of notes that she would have to wait until the morning to organize. Her burning eyes just wouldn't cooperate any longer.

As she filled a glass with ice cubes and raspberry juice, Vic went over countless options for press packets in her mind. Had she remembered correctly that Tiffany was studying to be a graphic artist? Certainly, that would be a talent she would want to call upon at some point in the near future.

Standing at the window in the dining room, she looked out over the low-slung buildings in the foreground toward the fading horizon in the distance, immediately recognizing the galloping canine silhouette against the shore.

A smile wound its way across her face as she spotted Louie's two companions, singling out the more masculine of them by the mane of thick hair that barely touched the collar of the bleached denim shirt he'd been wearing that afternoon. She lingered over the rhythm of his gait and the stature of his long, thin frame. Broad, muscular shoulders gave way to a thin waist and powerful legs that provided most of his height.

A strong and certain attraction had somehow imbedded itself within her during those hours of talking business with Drew, and Vic didn't need to bother to deny it now. She had distance and buildings and a good half-mile of sand to hide behind as she allowed herself the luxury of wading in her desire—temporarily. But as the moments ticked by and her fascination with him began to grow, gravitational pull threatened to draw her inner spirit straight across the space between them, and Vic quivered out of its grasp, turning her back on the setting sun and all that its reflection revealed.

Instead, she reached for the cigarette lying seductively on the table in front of her. Tracing its length between two fingers, she brought it to her mouth, stopping just short of actually touching her parted lips.

"No," she said aloud, and then tossed the thing back to the table with the jerk of her wrist.

Vic stalked into the kitchen and pulled the box of nicotine patches Krissy had sent from the shelf inside the cabinet, producing the folded paperwork from inside.

"Peel back the outer wrapper," she read aloud from the instructions, "and place the patch against the skin." Rolling her eyes, she did as she was told.

Chapter Seven

Vic couldn't remember a time when she'd been so worked up about an event that wasn't business-related. Not that Tiffany and Walter's engagement party was entirely social either, but Drew had warned her that it wouldn't be like any of the New York parties she'd ever attended, and she had the distinct feeling that he was right.

She'd gone out that afternoon in search of the perfect dress for the occasion and had felt certain she'd found it at a small shop located inside Tyrone Square Mall. It was a colorful number, the choice of which shocked even her, most of her apparel being of the more subdued variety in navy, black, gray, and assorted shades of tan.

Upon inspection of her reflection, she crinkled up her nose involuntarily, wondering if, at the age of 33, she could even carry off such a dress. Who did she think she was?

The cap-sleeved top of the dress was tame enough, at least in its corporate-issue color of black, and even its slight dip off her shoulders didn't reveal too much. But the billowing attached skirt with the tea-length hem was a tropical splash of bold color, a pallet for an array of all the reds, blues, greens, golds, and purples that she hadn't donned in years.

Vic slipped her feet into the black strappy sandals she'd purchased to go along with the dress and turned one ankle outward, examining the two-inch heel that screamed bright red, a shade perfectly matched by the enamel on her toenails.

She'd crimped sections of her jet-black hair with the iron she'd bought on impulse, bringing several strands together to one side with a delicate yet vibrant multi-colored barrette that had come as a set with six metal bracelets of the same varied hues. Vic almost didn't recognize the woman in the mirror, and a sudden twinge of insecure regret surged through her. It was too late to turn back now, she realized as she glanced at the clock on the bureau, but if time had permitted, she knew she

58

might have hopped straight into the shower to wash it all away and start again.

Drew's warning popped into her mind just then, and she grimaced at the memory.

"There won't be a classical quartet in the corner or champagne in crystal flutes," he had stated matter-of-factly. "Try to find something festive to wear."

The final suggestion was what had irked her the most. He'd said it as if he believed it was an impossible feat, but he thought he'd mention it just the same.

I can be festive, she thought rebelliously, summoning a certain dinner cruise she'd orchestrated just last summer to prove the point. It had been held to kick off the campaign for the newest designer fragrance, and she'd chosen a merry Mexican theme to lull guests into the mood. *Just because it was business doesn't mean it wasn't festive and carefree.*

Of course, the elegant A-line dress she'd worn that night might have been a stauncher choice than Drew Nolan would have made for her, but that was beside the point. Taking one last look in the mirror, she nodded. This would certainly show him!

Vic walked into the dining room and sat down on the chair in front of her laptop. Sliding one leg over the other, she clasped her hands together and folded them neatly into her lap.

Ten minutes to kill.

Acknowledging that this would be the time she'd normally spend indulging in a final smoke before leaving for her destination, Vic tapped her foot and stared straight ahead. After a few moments of that, her eyes casually meandered over to the table where, as she well knew, a lone cigarette sat enticingly immobile.

She looked away. And then glanced back.

An innocent sigh reminded her how pleasing it might be to inhale just a single draw of smoke into her lungs . . .

"Oh, phooey!" she exclaimed, and then leapt to her feet, grabbed her purse, and rushed out the door.

Louie barked a greeting as she pounded on Drew's door.

"Are you ready yet?" she snapped when he pulled it open,

but Drew just stood silent before her, his eyes wide with surprise. "Can we go?"

"I'm sorry," he said at last. "Do I know you?"

She grimaced, and then stared him down for a long moment. "You look . . . amazing."

"Yeah, yeah," she snarled. "You didn't know I had it in me. Do I have to wait all night for you?"

Drew's laughter evoked a bit of her own, and Vic felt the pressure on her heart beginning to lift.

"I'm sorry," she told him on a sigh. "I'm just a little tense. I'm trying . . . well . . . I'm trying to quit smoking."

"Oh!" he exclaimed. "That explains it. Well, come on in and have a glass of wine first. It will loosen you up."

"Unless you don't mind me lighting it on fire, I'm afraid you're setting yourself up for failure here."

Drew placed one hand on each of her shoulders and looked intently into her eyes before he guided her through the doorway.

"There's a bottle of wine in the fridge, and glasses hanging over the counter," he told her, gently pushing her along through the room. "I'm going to finish getting ready while you pour."

With a shrug, she wandered into the kitchen as he disappeared down the hall. She looked around the room for a moment, and then opened several drawers until she spotted the corkscrew.

"So, how long has it been since you had a cigarette?" he called out to her from the other room over the sound of Louie's continued barking. Then he added, "Louie! Can it!"

Vic glanced toward the dog at her feet and stuck her tongue out at him. Unexpectedly, he pinned back his ears and fell silent, wagging his tail emphatically.

"Day four," she returned, plucking a bottle of white zinfandel from several other choices in the rack inside the refrigerator.

"Vic, that's great!"

"It doesn't feel so great," she returned softly, stepping over Louie where he had spread out on the tile at her feet.

"I know it's hard, but it will be well worth it when you're completely nicotine-free," he told her. "I quit six years ago."

"You?" she exclaimed, pausing in her duties to glance toward the hallway down which he'd disappeared. "You were a smoker?"

"Since the age of sixteen," he responded. "And then my dad was diagnosed with lung cancer."

"Oh, that's right. I'm sorry," she said, and then poured two glasses of wine. Her own mother had succumbed to a form of bone cancer, and the memory squeezed at her heart for a moment.

"Yeah," Drew said as he entered the room and took one of the glasses from her hand. "That was quite a wake-up call. I figured I'd quit and show him how it was done."

"Did he ever stop smoking before he passed away?"

"He did. Better late than never, I guess. But it didn't change anything."

"I'm so sorry."

Raising his glass toward hers, Drew grinned. "Here's to Day Four of the battle. To the victor go the spoils."

Vic returned the smile half-heartedly, clinked her glass to his, and took a sip.

"Have you thought about trying a nicotine patch?" he asked her. "I've heard that can really help with the cravings."

Crinkling her nose, Vic lifted the cap sleeve of her dress to reveal a small white patch glued to the side of her arm.

"Oh. And how's that working for you?" he teased beneath a comical arch of his brow.

"Just great," she lied through her teeth. "I hardly think about it at all."

The pounding of music greeted them as Drew pulled into an empty spot near The Beachside Hut and shut off the motor. A free-standing sign by the door greeted them with the words: "Closed Tonight For Private Party. Congrats Tiffie & Walt "

Vic couldn't help but grin when the first people she saw as they walked through the front door were very much kindred spirits, two men in suits, their ties loosened and fruit-bearing drinks in their supple corporate hands. As they moved further in, Drew's hand at the small of her back guiding her through the crowd, the mix thickened. Vic's eyes moved from young party-goers with wild hair and assorted piercings to slightly older attendees looking as if they'd barely escaped Corporate America with their starched shirts intact.

A black woman with short curly braids and dressed in colorful African garb caught Vic's eye and then moved toward her bearing an absolutely luminous smile. She had a familiar twinkle in her chocolate brown eyes.

"You've got to be Vic," the woman roared above the music.

"Yes," she nodded, and then looked back to Drew, unsure.

"This is Penelope," he confirmed. "My best friend and fellow sunset aficionado."

"Oh!" Vic said on a grin, allowing Penelope to take both of her hands and pat them enthusiastically. "Good to meet you."

"I've got us a table," she shouted to Drew, pointing in a direction beyond the Jamaican band assembled on the small stage near the wall. "Back where the music isn't quite so ear-splitting."

"Follow Pen," Drew mouthed, and Vic did as she was told.

Before they reached the aforementioned table, Vic noticed Tiffany excitedly making her way toward her, arms outstretched, already engaged in conversation that wasn't making its way to her ears over the roar of the music. The spikes of her platinum-white hair were tipped with ruby-red glitter, as were her eyelids, both a perfect match to the sequins of the tube top which gathered several inches above a dangling belly button ring bearing a red crystal heart.

"I'm so glad you came!" she cried when she reached them, and Vic released a gasp of surprise when the girl wrapped her up in an embrace that nearly knocked the wind right out of her lungs. "You look positively gorgeous. Oh! And I want you to meet Walter!"

Vic inched her way through the throng, following the sleeve of Penelope's dashiki as Tiffany darted on to Drew, smothering his face in playful kisses and chattering fifty miles an hour in between them.

Penelope led the way through a curtain of beads into a smaller room housing a dozen or so tables, most of them occupied with more of the same incongruous crowd.

"We're over here," Penelope announced. "This is my son, Terrence, and his school chum, Omar."

"Pleased to meet you," Terrence greeted her, and Vic noticed there was no mistaking his resemblance to Penelope.

"What would you like to drink?" Penelope asked.

"Oh, I don't know," she replied, inspecting the tropical extravaganza on the table in front of her hostess. "What are you having?"

"A fruit concoction of some kind," she explained with a shrug, and then turned to her son. "Get one for Andrew as well."

Terrence rose to his feet just as Drew appeared, and the two of them embraced amiably and exchanged a few words before Terrence made his way back through the beaded screen.

"Omar, good to see you again," Drew exclaimed, and the two shook hands vigorously before Drew dropped down into the chair next to Vic.

"I see you've been marked," Penelope said to Drew, motioning to his face.

Dusting his fingers across his cheek in confusion, Drew shrugged and looked at Vic questioningly.

"Oh!" she giggled, and then reached for a napkin and began wiping away the traces of welcome from his face. "Tiffany's lipstick," she told him, and Drew groaned and softly rolled his eyes as she continued.

When the final lip print was nearly erased, Vic got caught in the current of Drew's gaze, and he seemed to hold her there against her will for what felt like an hour.

"Is it my color, at least?" he asked her in a tone far too seductive to endure.

"Nah," she sputtered at last, dragging her focus from him and tossing the used napkin down on the table with a jerk. "You're more summer than autumn."

"I'll bear that in mind."

Vic thought she caught a glimmer of a smile on Penelope, but the older woman covered it well by focusing on the table before her.

Terrence appeared that very moment, balancing several drinks on a tray which also brimmed with bunches of grapes, a couple wedges of cheese, a small cup of spinach dip and an assortment of crackers.

"Leave it to my boy to find the food," Penelope declared.

And while the others busied themselves with transferring the spread to the table before them, Vic used the time to slow her heart back down to its rightful rhythm.

"As most everyone in this room is probably aware, I wasn't among the first to get onboard with this particular romance."

Laughter popped around the room, and the conservative man with the microphone at the center of the stage playfully silenced them with his hand. The top few buttons of his shirt were undone and his sleeves were rolled casually to the elbow. What once had been a perfectly-knotted silk tie now hung around his collar like an ascot.

"I know, I know," he said with a chuckle, "but since I'm now going to be the best man at their wedding, you can forgive me for being so, so wrong."

Spontaneous applause ignited from the crowd surrounding the stage, and Vic grinned as Drew added to the clamor with a piercing whistle that stung her ears.

"Let me tell you what made me finally come around," the best man announced. "Let me tell you what made me fall in love with Tiffie, just as Walter had."

Vic noticed Tiffany gently take the hand of the man beside her, the man she now realized was the girl's intended groom.

Walter was rather handsome, in an accountant-chic sort of way. His dark brown eyes were set off by a short-cropped head of wavy hair of the same color, and tortoiseshell glasses completed the picture of a high school nerd, all grown up into his potential. There was no denying the smile of contentment that radiated from him at the mere touch of his future bride, and Vic's heart squeezed a little at the sight.

"I've known him since college," the man continued, and Vic dragged her attention back to center stage. "There wasn't a guy on campus who was more focused, more intense than my buddy, Walter. After mid-terms, when the rest of us were getting a little loose, letting off some steam, Walter could be found at the campus bookstore, trying to get in ahead of the line for books for the next semester's classes."

"Now that I can believe," Drew joked softly to Vic, leaning in close as he did.

"I'll never forget one night, when the rest of us were heading out to look for some trouble, and I was trying my hardest to persuade Walter to come along. 'Put on your dancing shoes, for once,' I said to him. 'Let's get a little crazy.' And he turned to me and said, 'Stu. I don't own a pair of dancing shoes. And what's more, I haven't owned a pair of them in my whole miserable life.'"

Moans and groans of sympathy popped up from various corners of the room, and then someone shouted, "You coulda lent him yours, Stu. You've got a few to spare!" And it was followed by the amused laughter of those who obviously knew it to be true.

"I didn't have to lend him mine," Stu told them seriously. "Because one night, not so long ago, Walter reminded me of that conversation. And he said to me, 'Stuie, my friend. I've finally found my dancing shoes. And I'm going to marry her before she wises up and bossa novas right out of my life.'"

Applause erupted one more time, as an obviously-moved Tiffany threw her arms around Walter's neck and planted a passionate kiss right on his lips.

"Raise your punch glasses, friends," Stu called to them when they were through. "And drink with me to Walter and Tiffie. My stiff-necked buddy, and the wind beneath his wingtips."

Drew reached over just then and clinked his glass to Vic's, and the two of them toasted the happy couple, along with the rest of the room brimming full with well-wishers.

"To Walter and Tiffany," Drew hooted, and the applause and howls of the surrounding guests chimed in with sentiments of their own.

Resisting the rising lump in her throat, Vic downed several gulps from the fruit punch and forced a smile onto her face to replace what she knew had nearly given way to a contortion of raw emotion.

Chapter Eight

It took several waiters to wheel out the wicker cart bearing the sheet cake. It was a red velvet creation with cream cheese icing, garnished on all sides by enormous chocolate-dipped strawberries. A procession of waitresses followed, carrying cake plates and forks in one hand and glittering sparklers reminiscent of an Independence Day celebration in the other.

"The boys will fetch the cake," Penelope said as the crowd began to disperse and the band kicked in with a generic tropical rhythm. "Why don't you two dance."

"Oh . . . no . . ." Vic objected.

"It's a great idea," Drew interrupted, taking her by the hand and dragging her out to the floor where a half dozen other couples had already congregated.

"No, Drew, really . . ."

"Hey," he said, placing his hands on both of her shoulders and looking her squarely in the eye, "we had a deal, didn't we?"

"What are you talking about?"

"You were going to try and loosen up a little, remember? Nothing loosens up a corporate tiger like a dance floor and a nice Caribbean beat."

"I'm here," she offered. "And I didn't dress the part of a corporate tiger."

"And a lovely effort it is," Drew acknowledged with a grin. "You look positively . . ."

"Festive?" she asked.

"Why, yes. Festive."

"But what about you?" she challenged him. "You were going to meet me halfway in this operation of change."

"And I will. First thing tomorrow morning, in the office. But tonight," he exclaimed, twirling her by the hand with a dramatic flair, "we *dahnce!*"

Vic looked back at him for a long moment, her arm suspended in the air above their heads, held there by the silliest man she had ever met. The sight of him, so hopeful and insistent, curled her face into a rebellious, uncontrollable smile.

"One dance," she warned him.

Drew wasted no time in sweeping her into his arms and taking full advantage of her momentary surrender, the rhythmic sway of his body against hers bringing a mist of perspiration to every inch of her flesh. Every once in a while, he would take her by the hand and fling her away from him, but just as she would catch her breath, he would reel her back in, swooping her up in his strong arms once more.

It had been a long time since Vic had been held by a man. She'd nearly forgotten what it was like. And this man, in particular, did things to her, brought reactions churning to the surface, like no other had ever done before. She wanted to attribute this sudden reaction to their divergent personalities; certainly, the differences between them were as vast and far-reaching as opposing cultures from contrasting sides of the globe. And the old adage did proclaim that "opposites attract!" But whatever it was that was going on between she and Drew on this particular evening, Vic sensed that it ran far deeper than mere attraction. And that was what frightened her most of all.

Don't start decorating him with romantic hearts and flowers like the ones on the stupid cake, she warned herself as he spun her out one more time. *This is business. And mixing business with other things can never result in anything good.*

But then she was wrapped in his arms once more, and the thoughts flew straight out of her head.

"I'm afraid we're going to have to say goodnight," Vic told Tiffany, leaning across the table to give the girl a quick hug. "I had the best time!"

"I'm so glad you came," Walter told her from Tiffany's side. "I don't know what you two have planned, but Tiffie tells me you're instrumental in what she's got going for this surprise of a wedding."

"There aren't many grooms so willing to give their brides *carte blanche* the way you have," Vic grinned. "I admire your courage."

Walter considered that for a moment, and then smiled. "Whatever makes her happy. As long as I don't end up in traction instead of Costa Rica for my honeymoon, it's all right with me."

"Walter, you've got yourself a peach of a girl," Drew interjected, and the two of them shook hands enthusiastically.

"Don't I know it."

"You two make an awesome couple," Tiffany told Drew while motioning toward Vic. "You were tearing up that dance floor!"

Vic's eyes darted downward, and she found herself biting the side of her lip until it ached.

We're not a couple, she wanted to point out, but then thought better of it.

"Thanks again for inviting me," she said instead. "Give me a call in a couple of days and we'll talk." Then, mouthing the words secretively, she added, "About the dress!"

"I can't wait!" Tiffany squealed, and the girl took her hand and squeezed it one last time before letting her go.

Several more good-byes were offered before they finally reached the door, and the night air felt wonderful and crisp as it greeted her.

Vic enjoyed the drive home that night with the convertible top down, and the wind blowing what was left of the crimped curls from her hair. Some form of soft jazz whispered from the radio, and the moon was casting a silver orb of light straight down on the glassy bay in the distance. She breathed in a sturdy lungful of it, as if taking in the whole of the night rather than just the air around it. She closed her eyes as she released it, slowly and with the slightest twinge of regret.

"Walter and Tiffany are quite the pair, aren't they?" Drew broke the silence.

"They're actually kind of sweet together," she admitted.

"Well, you know what they say. Opposites attract."

Vic darted a glance toward him, wondering for a moment if he'd been able to read her mind earlier in the evening, and then dismissed the notion with great relief.

"Not usually, though," she commented. "Not in the real world."

"And what constitutes the real world?"

"Different things to different people," she replied. "For me, it's New York and my work. The subway and Wall Street. For you, I'd guess it includes a marketable idea of romance and the occasional sunset walk with Penelope."

"And never the twain shall meet?"

"Only temporarily," she told him.

Drew breathed out a gust of amusement before replying. "You said that so quickly. Not even a second thought."

"There's no room for second thoughts in my world, Drew. Things move quickly, and it's important to keep up."

Drew rounded the corner into the lot in front of their building, and eased the gearshift to park before turning off the key. Without warning, he turned to her, cautiously reaching out and smoothing a stray lock of hair back from her face.

"Then you'd better get running again," he said on a whisper. "I wouldn't want you to slow down on my account."

Vic's eyes grew wide for a moment, locked into his against her will.

"I had a good time tonight," she told him truthfully.

"So did I."

"But let's not mistake it for something it wasn't."

"Enlighten me," he said softly. "What was it?"

"It was a moment in time," she replied sadly.

"Then I'll do this quickly. Before the moment has passed."

Before she could process his words, his hands gently encircled her neck and drew her to him. His warm lips covered hers, softly at first, and then with more intensity. Closing her eyes, she succumbed, and her head dropped back gently against his hand, allowing his fingers to tangle themselves deeply into her wind-mussed hair.

It was a kiss that movie romances were made of. If she'd been standing, she felt certain she might have bent her knee involuntarily, lifting her leg slightly in a manner given to on-screen goddesses and femme fatales throughout the ages.

"No, Drew," she protested suddenly, pressing against his chest with both of her hands as logic made its way through her brain and reality reared its ugly, mostly-unwelcomed head.

"Why?" he asked her with a sleepy look to him.

"Because we can't."

She was firmer now in her resolve, and he obviously sensed it, pulling back and looking at her dreamily, much like someone yanked from the edge of a very deep sleep.

"Why?" he repeated.

"You know why," she replied.

Drew blinked thoughtfully, and then pulled back further. Yes, he did know why. She could see that he did.

Placing her palm gently against his cheek, Vic tried to smile.

"It was a beautiful moment in time, though," she told him honestly. "The whole evening."

"But the moment has passed?" he asked her regretfully.

"I'm sorry."

"I'm sorry, too."

Vic pulled herself together and slid out of the car. She was at the bottom of the stairs before she looked back to find Drew still sitting behind the wheel of his car, watching her.

"Good night."

"Good night," he replied, but made no move to follow.

Vic peeled the tiny patch from her arm and tossed it to the counter. In the same motion, she began opening kitchen drawers, one after the other.

"Where are they!" she squealed aloud. "Where are they?"

The memory rubbed against her flesh like raw silk, and she hurried into the dining room and shuffled the papers scattered on the table until she found what she was looking for.

"Oh, thank you, God," she said with a sigh, sinking down into the chair as she tapped a cigarette from the pack and popped it between her lips.

A hearty groan worked its way up from inside her and escaped along with the first blessed exhale. This was no time to try and quit smoking! What in the world had she been thinking?

Vic drew in another lungful and held it there a moment before releasing it slowly, delightfully. With eyes closed, she let out another soft moan of ecstasy.

"Ooooohhh, yeaaaah."

Nothing so good should be so bad for a person.

Vic opened her eyes and stared out the window at the flicker of lights in the distance. One moment of bliss had led her to another, and she hopped to her feet when she realized that her mind had darted back to Drew's kiss before she'd even realized it. She paced back and forth in front of the window several times, puffing away at the only solace she could find, trying to shove the memory from her stubborn brain, but it didn't appear to be going anywhere.

Oh, why did I let him kiss me that way? she wondered, shuddering beneath the thick fog of the moment that still cloaked her like a possessive shroud. *Some things are just better left to the imagination.*

But Vic knew far too much now, and an overwhelming fear grabbed hold of her just then. What if she could never forget? What if the velvet smoothness of his lips never left her, if it somehow remained engrained upon her memory with the same stark intensity it held now?

She remembered the cigarette perched limply between her two fingers and took another draw from it. She could still taste him beneath the bitter lure of the tobacco, and she cursed him for it.

"Drew," she said out loud, practicing what she would say to him, "something like that can never happen between us again."

And she would mean it! She would make him believe that she meant it, at least. And then perhaps her own resolve would follow suit.

"My purpose here is strictly business," she continued out loud. "Anything else beyond that is completely out of the question. And frankly, I'm going to hold you responsible for keeping your distance from me. Any further physical contact shall be strictly prohibited."

I sound like a legal contract, she chastised herself as she took another drag from her cigarette.

Her thoughts were interrupted by a quiet rap at the front door, and Vic jumped at the transition. Stamping out the fire at the end of the cigarette with one hand, she fanned the smoke from the air with the other.

"Who is it?" she articulated between frantic puffs of air sent upward to break through the residual cloud.

"It's Drew. Can I talk to you a minute? I saw your lights."

Vic poked the cigarette stub into the pack from which it had come, and quickly tucked it down into her purse.

"Just a minute," she replied, waving her arms at the telltale haze as she made her way slowly toward the front door. "Come on in," she said through a pasted-on smile when she opened it to greet him.

"Thanks," he muttered, and then passed through the doorway with his face downward.

"I'm actually glad you stopped by," she told him.

"Are you smoking again?"

"What?" she exclaimed guiltily. "No. Why?"

"You'll probably want to air this place out then, or the left-over nicotine is going to be a killer on your willpower."

"Yeah," she replied softly. "I'll do that."

"Listen, about tonight," he began, and then paused to run his hands through his hair in what she had come to recognize as a telltale sign of distress. "I owe you an apology."

"No, no," she interjected. "I shouldn't have led you to believe that it was acceptable to . . ."

"I mean, maybe it was the romantic atmosphere, or the festivities in general—"

"Or the moonlit bay—"

"Yeah, or maybe just the way your hair was blown by the wind—"

"Anyway . . ." they added simultaneously, and then each chuckled in response.

"Anyway," Drew repeated, "I'm sorry. And it won't ever happen again, I promise you."

Something akin to disappointment dropped inside Vic's chest, but she was determined to ignore it for the moment.

"Yes, thank you," she replied. "I appreciate that."

When she looked up into his eyes, she saw something unexpected there to greet her. A sort of amusement, mixed with stunned surprise.

"What?"

"Oh, nothing," he answered strangely. "Are you sure you haven't been smoking again?"

"No," she insisted anxiously. "Why do you keep asking me that?"

"No reason. Except that, well, your purse seems to be on fire."

Vic spun around on her heel, horrified to find that, indeed, her purse had ignited with a small billow of smoke.

"Oh!" she exclaimed, rushing toward it frantically, then retrieved a dish towel to beat it down to a manageable level. As soon as she was able, she picked the thing up by the strap, flung it around her, and rushed it into the kitchen sink.

Vic flicked on the faucet and ran a stream of water over the bag. When she turned around, she saw Drew cautiously grounding out an ember that had fallen to the carpet near the table with the tip of his shoe. When he looked up, her eyes darted away from his in embarrassment, and when she looked back again he was standing mere inches behind her.

"You know, just a tip," he said softly, picking up the discarded nicotine patch from the counter next to the sink. "These usually work better if you actually wear them."

Vic emerged from her apartment the next morning to find a bright red fire extinguisher leaning against the jamb of her door. A hot wave of crimson humiliation flowed over her, and the events of the prior evening resonated in her memory.

"Very funny," she said aloud as she moved the thing inside the door and closed it behind her. "What a funny guy."

Vic had awoken that morning with a new plan.

Well, actually, it's back to my old plan, she had thought confidently to herself. *All work, all the time. If something proves effective for you, you stick with it.*

She'd used her morning shower as a metaphor to drive the point home—washing that man right out of her hair, and all that. Every little part of her morning ritual was performed with new resolve for a fresh start and a focus on completing the task at hand. She had come to Florida to perform a miracle, and perform it she would!

Drew's little joke had ignited a simple reminder of the night before, and it had been a momentary setback at best, she promised herself. She took each of the concrete stairs with a thud of determination. She discarded the charred remains of her evening bag into the Dumpster as she rounded the corner, then stepped into the office with a boldness that surprised even her.

Louie greeted her with his usual tirade, but Vic proceeded beyond him without a second glance.

"Can it!" Drew called out from the office beyond the conference room, and the dog mumbled a few parting shots before disappearing in his direction.

Vic plopped down into her regular chair at the conference table and began organizing herself for the day. Once her laptop was set up, she signed online and opened the first of six waiting e-mails.

"Morning," Drew greeted her from the doorway, propping himself against it as if he were needed to hold it up.

"Morning," she returned casually, then focused in on the screen before her.

"Do you want some coffee?"

"If there's any made," she replied without averting her attention.

A steaming cup was set before her moments later, and she mumbled a quick thank you as she moved on to the next e-mail in the file.

"Check out Marchant's newest client," Krissy had written, and Vic clicked on the button to download the attachment.

She chuckled out loud as the graphic appeared. A new and improved nicotine patch, guaranteed to drastically reduce cigarette cravings.

"Send me a box," she wrote in reply. "Or maybe send a dozen."

The last e-mail waiting was the one she'd been hoping to find, and she eagerly clicked it open.

"What you've described sounds like a great opportunity,"

Sasha wrote. "Do you want to come to me, or shall I come to you?"

"Excellent!" she exclaimed aloud. "Now that's what I wanted to hear!"

"What is?"

She spun around to find Drew standing behind her, a box of computer paper in his arms.

"Why are you hovering?" she asked, shooting him a little frown.

"I am not hovering," he replied, irritation creeping up over his features like an impending storm. "My printer is out of paper. This is where I keep it."

"Oh. The designer I asked to help out with Tiffany's dress," she explained, "has agreed."

"Great." His enthusiasm was a bit lackluster for Vic's taste.

"Yes, it is great," she told him, sliding one leg over the other and pausing to take a sip from her cup of coffee. "It will be great for Tiffany, of course, but it will also be great for your business."

"How so?"

"We're going to make this wedding a floating advertisement for Romantic Overture," she informed him. "We're going to take video of everything involved, from the engagement party the other night to the honeymoon, and then we're going to have it featured anywhere I can sell it. It's called creating a buzz."

Drew nodded faintly, and then shook his head as he walked out of the office without a word. The whole idea was obviously lost on him, Vic realized.

No matter, she thought excitedly. *He'll be thrilled when he sees the end result.*

"Sasha!" she exclaimed into the receiver a moment later. "Victoria Townsend. I'm so pleased to have you onboard."

Drew couldn't make out the exact verbiage, he could only sense the general high energy of the conversation. The hum of her enthusiasm irritated him somehow, and he scolded himself for it, taking great pains to remind himself that Vic's zeal was a commodity he desperately needed to covet.

She must know what she's doing, he thought, and then couldn't help but wonder what it was going to cost him in dollars and cents.

"Do you have a company credit card?" she asked suddenly from the doorway.

Perfect timing. Now's the time, Nolan. Speak up.

"I do," he replied in a monotone that sounded rather droll, even to his own ears.

She waited for a moment, and then asked, "Well, can I have the number? I have to get Sasha a flight."

"I don't think my company card is going to help you in that respect," he finally admitted. "Unless her flight is under a hundred and forty-six bucks."

Chapter Nine

"I don't understand."

Drew ran both of his hands through his hair, then leaned back and looked at Vic seriously. "That's what's left of my credit limit."

"You're joking."

"Well, there are funds I can draw on," he explained, discomfort coursing its way through every vein and every artery. "It's just that I didn't manage to acquire them until . . . well, the card company isn't willing to extend any further credit to me right now, so I saw no sense in—"

"Okay, Drew," Vic interrupted, sitting down on the corner of his desk. "I'm going to need a complete rundown of your financial picture before we go any further."

The thought that he could draw her that picture with a couple of crayons and a piece of construction paper fluttered across his mind.

"Why don't you bring your books and join me in the conference room," she suggested. "Let's get this sorted out."

Drew spent the rest of the afternoon in relative silence, sitting across from her like a child awaiting punishment to be handed down by the school principal.

So what's it going to be? he thought bitterly as he watched her poring over his checkbook register, comparing the entries to the account log. *Detention? What? C'mon, boss lady. Let's get to it.*

"Alright," she finally said, breaking the quell like shattered glass. "Things don't look so bad. It's not hopeless. We just have to make a few minor adjustments."

"What kind of adjustments?" he asked suspiciously.

"The first thing we'll do is arrange a line of credit."

"I told you, the card company isn't going to—"

"There's more than one credit card company out there, Drew," she interjected. "Your recent history with them isn't ex-

78

actly stellar. If I were American Express, I wouldn't extend you any favors either. But there are other institutions that offer—"

"I've applied for other credit cards, Vic. I've been shut down by every one of them."

"I understand that," she replied patiently. "We'll just take another route. You've got almost twenty thousand dollars in cash sitting in an account right now. We can take half of that and arrange for a secured credit card for business purposes, and then put the rest in a money market account where it will at least be working for you while it's sitting there."

Drew didn't like admitting that he was torn in half by both humiliation and admiration. He really wasn't the dolt she was seeing at the moment, and he didn't enjoy needing this irritating woman to sort out his financial affairs. Nor did he particularly relish the idea of letting her camp out on every square inch of what was left of his privacy. Yet she did seem to have a surprisingly firm grasp on a situation that had incessantly eluded him for months on end.

Drew resisted the sudden urge to explain himself, to tell her that he'd always been more of a creative type than anything else. He had talents and skills, after all! They just didn't fall at the business end of the spectrum.

It wasn't like his personal affairs were in tatters like his father's business, after all. This was what he'd been left with, and getting his mind around how to save a failing business that he hadn't really wanted in the first place had proved more than a little challenging. Taking out a second mortgage on his family home in hopes of saving it was a last-ditch effort on behalf of his father, and if it failed . . . Well, Drew couldn't allow himself to think in those terms. It couldn't fail. That was why he'd gone to Trent for help. That was why he was sitting here now, praying that a pit bull with amazing blue eyes could find the answers that he couldn't.

"Look, don't feel bad about this," Vic said softly, as if she could read his mind. "Not everyone has a head for this part of running a business. You have your talents, and I have mine. This just happens to be one of mine. We'll take care of it, and that will be that. Frankly, I'm pleasantly surprised to see that there's something there to build from. I've seen your records for the last year of business, and it certainly didn't reflect this kind of net. Where did you dig up your financial base?"

"Weapons," he replied dryly. "I run them in and out of the country for Castro. It's a very lucrative sideline."

Vic narrowed her sky-blue eyes at him with a smirk. "Well, keep it up," she suggested finally. "And if things don't work out the way I want them to, I might make a run or two with you myself."

Don't even joke about failure, Drew found himself thinking as he stared back at her. *You're my final shot at bringing this business out of the toilet.*

"Are you hungry?" she asked him out of the blue. "I'm starved. How about we order in Chinese?"

"You go ahead," he replied. "I've got somewhere to be."

And that somewhere was calling to him like the strange and eerie howl of a wolf in the distance. Twenty minutes later, Drew pulled his car down the long paved driveway that he had once known so well.

Throwing the gear into park, he leaned back into the leather seat and stared at the large stone house before him. He'd hardly visited his family home since the rainy afternoon of his father's funeral, but not a single thing ever seemed to change besides the accumulation of leaves and grasses blown against the front door.

A block of emotion sat on his chest like bricks, and Drew felt weary beneath the weight of it as he pulled himself out of the car. He gazed momentarily at the brass plaque above the doorbell.

The Nolan Abode. Established 1978.

His mother had only enjoyed three years, before her death, in the house she and his father had so lovingly and painstakingly built together, but she'd managed to make the most of every moment she'd had. In the end, though, her heart just wasn't what it should have been, and she succumbed to its weariness, leaving father and son to cope with the reality of living without her.

Drew ambled slowly around the side of the house. The massive banyan tree up on the hill looked like an old friend to him, and he stepped up his pace as he approached it. Known for their fort-like growth patterns, Drew wondered how many days and nights he'd spent suspended within those branches, hiding out inside the maze of its trunk.

He'd made a lot of plans, dreamed a lot of dreams, in the arms of that old friend. It was there that he'd devised the scheme that would finally result in snagging his first date; he'd practiced inviting Trisha Norris to the 7th grade dance for hours on end within those branches. And later, when he'd been caught up by the fleeting notion that carpentry—and then later, architecture—might be something he'd like to pursue as a career, it was the chunky wood of the banyan tree that had inspired him. Funny how so many of his dreams like that one had unwillingly fallen by the wayside in the years that followed.

His eyes meandered over the grass that surrounded the tree, landing finally on the two lone headstones at the plateau of the hill. He approached them cautiously, trepidation squeezing his heart as he did.

Francine Elizabeth Nolan, the first one read. *April 10, 1939–November 21, 1981. Beloved Wife & Treasured Mother.*

Drew ran his fingertips along the arch of the stone, and then moved on to the second one.

Fisher Andrew Nolan, December 6, 1937–May 16, 2002. Father & Friend.

Drew followed the letters of the words with his eyes until tears blurred them. He used the back of his hand to wipe away the moisture, then sat down in the dry grass between the two headstones. He glanced out across the yard to the back of the house, noticing some loose branches cluttering the veranda.

That would have driven Dad nuts, he thought, and a bittersweet smile tickled the corner of his mouth.

Making a mental note to do some clean-up work before he drove back to town, Drew folded his legs and then leaned back against the stone marking his father's grave. Anxiety, buried so deep within him that it almost stung as it made its way upward, came out in the form of a somber, vibrating sigh.

"Ah, Dad," he said with a whisper. "I just hope I don't end up letting you down."

Vic placed the last of the placards down on the table in front of her and smiled at Sasha.

"My gosh, these are so beautiful," she breathed, leaning back against the hard wood of the chair.

"Is there anything there you think will suit Tiffany?"

Vic grinned. "Well," she began, and then paused to take a sip from the mineral water before her. "Tiffany is a very unique individual. And although your designs are clearly unique as well, I'm not quite sure—" Her voice broke off as a knock at the hotel room door drew their attention. "Well, you can see for yourself."

Vic pulled open the door with a flourish, as if presenting royalty, and focused intently on Sasha's face as Tiffany waltzed in. She wasn't disappointed when the designer's eyes widened and then froze there, her mouth gaping open in a perfectly round little *O*.

Tiffany's stark white hair was tousled in all directions, tipped and streaked with something black that took on the sheen of enamel. Her blackened eyes looked cat-like as she smiled, and her charcoal-tinted lips turned upward to form a scallop beneath her pert, gem-embellished nose.

"Tiffany Breckenridge," Vic announced, "meet Sasha Rollins, your wedding dress designer."

"I am so thrilled to meet you," Tiffany sang as she approached and took Sasha's hand into hers, shaking it frantically. "This is such a cool thing you're doing. Not just for me, but for Vic and Drew and the business. I mean, I just can't tell you how awesome I think it is. I almost can't believe you're here."

Without warning, Tiffany threw her arms around the woman's neck and embraced her enthusiastically.

"Oh!" Sasha exclaimed. "Well, it's . . . nice to meet you, too."

The designer gazed into Vic's eyes over the slope of

Tiffany's shoulder and cracked an absurd little smile, punctuated with the arch of her brow.

"Tiffany, Sasha's brought along some sketches for you to take a look at," Vic said as she led the way to the table at the corner of the suite. "Now, they're beautiful gowns, but I'm not sure I was successful in expressing to her how really non-traditional you are. So take a look, and we'll get some ideas, and work from there."

Sasha twisted her long curls around her fist and tossed them behind her head as she scuffed the chair closer to the table. One by one, she displayed the sketches to Tiffany, and each of the gowns was met with gasps of admiration.

"This might be something we can build from," Sasha told her as she showed her the next in line. "It has a halter bodice supported by embroidered and beaded double straps. The skirt is a fully shirred, multi-layered tulle, embellished with clear sequins and rocals."

"It's awesome," Tiffany said with a sigh.

"Or this next one," Sasha continued. "This is silk organza and satin. The bodice is fitted and decorated with squashed appliqué roses. The hem of the full organza skirt is edged in satin."

"Beautiful. Just beautiful."

"And the last one is a charmeuse gown," she told her. "Silver-lined beads form the pattern above the inverted V-shaped waistline."

"I wonder if we could do a W-shaped instead," Tiffany suggested seriously, and then looked to Vic for confirmation.

"I'm not sure you want to do that with the waistline," Vic offered. "It might not be very flattering."

"Oh. Okay."

When they had reached the last of more than a dozen sketches, Tiffany shook her head wildly.

"These are just the most beautiful dresses," she told Sasha sincerely. "Just awesome." Then, turning to Vic, she softly added, "But I don't really see anything that screams, 'Me!' "

"Well," Sasha began, exchanging a quick glance with Vic.

"Why don't you tell me what you had in mind and we'll see what we can do?"

"Okay!" she exclaimed, then quickly produced a large folded envelope from her bag and emptied its contents out onto the table.

Several dozen magazine cut-outs fluttered into an unorganized collage between them, and Tiffany pulled one of the full-color pictures from the pile. The two-piece ensemble displayed was bright purple with a tight strapless top with bare midriff and a mini-skirt so snug that it bunched around the middle.

"O-kay," Sasha commented without expression.

"Walter likes my belly button," Tiffany explained. "I was thinking something that shows it off might really make him happy."

Vic could hardly contain the laughter that pressed on her lungs, she bit down on both of her lips in an effort to suppress its release.

"O-kay," the designer repeated. "Why don't we start with the basics. Were you thinking of wearing a white dress, or did you want something more non-traditional for your gown?"

"Oh, no, I want white," Tiffany told her, wide-eyed. "But I don't want one of those church trains or a bunch of layers of meringue. That's just not me."

"Yes," Sasha agreed. "I believe you're right. Let's have a look at the other pictures you've brought along."

"And we're getting married on the beach, so it has to be something short. Oh, and I want to be barefoot. Will that be a problem?"

"Umm, no, that shouldn't be a—"

"Awesome! And I was thinking we could incorporate the whole W-theme into the dress somehow. Did Vic tell you that it's a W-themed wedding?"

"I think she did mention—"

"So maybe we could use beads or rhinestones or something, and cover the dress in little W's. Oh, or do a neckline in the shape of a W! That would be so cool! Could we do that?"

Vic slipped one leg over the other and leaned back in her

chair. She speculated about how long it had been after Tiffany's arrival that Sasha had undoubtedly begun to wonder just what in the world she had gotten herself into.

Just remember, she thought as she watched the frozen expression on her friend Sasha's face. *The pay-off comes after everyone in America sees what you were able to do under this kind of challenge.*

While the two of them exchanged ideas—or at least Tiffany offered them while Sasha studied her new client cautiously— Vic grabbed the camera she'd brought along and began snapping photographs of the women at work.

Framing Tiffany in the viewfinder, she found herself smiling as Sasha suggested, "Maybe we could go with a little more length to the skirt. Not too much, just enough to maintain an air of elegance to the affair."

She snapped the photograph just as Tiffany responded with a confused cock of her head.

Now that's the money shot, she thought, then couldn't resist chuckling right out loud.

Vic pulled her rental car next to Drew's convertible in the parking lot and shut off the key just in time to see Penelope walking toward her.

"Hey! Good to see you again," she greeted the woman with a smile.

"You, too. Drew tells me you've spent the afternoon going over wedding gown possibilities with Tiffany and your designer friend. You must be exhausted."

"It was kind of fun, actually," Vic replied as she slid out of the car. "If anyone's exhausted, I'd say it's Sasha."

"Tiffany can be quite a surprise the first time you meet her," Penelope commented knowingly.

"Yes. She certainly can."

"We're planning to have dinner down at the beach tonight," she added casually. "Care to join us?"

"Oh, no, thank you. I don't want to intrude."

"It's no intrusion at all," Penelope said insistently. "I'm

bringing grilled chicken fingers and some of my famous slaw, and the sunset will be showing up for after-dinner entertainment. You must come."

Vic hesitated for a moment, and then smiled. "You know, it does sound like fun. What time?"

"The eats come out around six-thirty. Drew will show you the way."

"Thanks, Penelope. I appreciate the invitation."

"Well, you can't spend all your time in Florida eating take-out food and being stuck in that office."

"I can't?" Vic joked.

"No. You can't. I'll see you at six-thirty."

Vic walked into the office, and Louie silently greeted her with the wag of his tail.

"What's with you?" she asked the dog happily. "Aren't you going to bark at me?"

"He's used to you now," Drew replied as he sauntered out of his office and into the reception area. "Don't encourage him."

Vic grinned as she tapped Louie's head tenderly.

"How did it go with Tiffany?"

"She's given Sasha a lot to think about, that's for sure," she answered.

"I'll bet."

Drew slipped several pink squares of paper out of the divider at the edge of the reception desk and handed them to Vic.

"Phone messages," he told her.

"Oh, thanks."

She flicked through them quickly.

"Krissy," she muttered, and then moved on to the next one. "Devon?"

Her pulse kicked into double time as she looked at Drew in horror.

"Devon McKay called?"

Taking the slip of paper from her fingers, he glanced at it and nodded. "That's what it says here," he quipped, and then handed it back to her.

"Well, what did he want?"

"He wanted to talk to you," he stated matter-of-factly. "I said you weren't here. He asked if you would call him. I said yes. That was the extent of it."

"Oh."

"So, who is he?"

"No one."

"Well, did No One come back from the dead or something?"

"No, no," Vic said, forcing an unwilling smile to her face in an effort to keep the bad news from Drew for as long as possible. A call from Devon McKay always meant bad news.

Devon was the associate producer for *Tying the Knot,* a show which had premiered three years back to very little notice. It was just one of a hundred other cable shows taking up airtime in the middle of the day while the networks were running their soap operas. And then something fortuitously tragic had occurred. While filming an episode surrounding the upcoming wedding of pop star Erikka, an unfortunate bus accident had taken the lives of everyone aboard. *Knot's* four-man film crew had died alongside Erikka and six others from her entourage.

When the hype began to expand beyond its own borders, and even the most industrious reporters had run out of tidbits about the pop star's life and times to keep their rags in the know, the spotlight began to bleed over and *Tying the Knot* was thrust to center stage. It was faster than setting an egg timer. Public sympathy and the well-oiled machine that is public relations had harmoniously combined to create a mega-hit for Jersey South Productions.

They had developed and honed their often-copied-but-never-duplicated entertainment magazine format over the last decade with a string of hit television shows. And when the opportunity presented itself, their executives had plucked a struggling little cable show out of the throng and backed it for everything they were worth. What emerged was a slick and polished thirty-minute weekly primetime extravaganza featuring the wedding process of anybody-who-is-anybody, a coveted little production which generated ratings as well as advertising dollars that would make a grown television executive weep with joy.

In order for Romantic Overtures to make her well-planned leap from local nothing to national something, Vic needed a feature commitment from *Tying the Knot*. But a call from Devon McKay was not a good sign. He was known as The Axe. The call came from him when someone was about to be disappointed, and Vic wasn't in the mood to be disappointed.

She glanced at her watch. Devon would be out of his office by this time. It looked like The Axe was going to have to strike tomorrow instead. It was going to be a very long night, she predicted. Waiting was never her strong suit.

"Well," Drew replied thoughtfully, bringing Vic back to the moment with a thud. "I'm headed out for a while. I'll see you later."

She shook her head abruptly and tossed the messages to the desktop.

"Are you going to meet Penelope?" she asked.

"Yes, we're having dinner down at the—"

"I know," she interrupted. "I mean, I'm going, too."

When Drew's eyebrows knit together questioningly, she added, "She invited me."

"When?"

"Just a little while ago, outside."

"Oh."

"If you'd rather I didn't go—"

"No, no," he assured her awkwardly. "It's fine. I didn't know she . . . Well, let's go then."

"Can I run upstairs and change first?"

"Put a motor on it then," he said, nodding toward the door. "Pen's chicken fingers wait for no man."

"Give me five minutes."

Vic threw on a pair of jeans and a black knit halter she'd picked up the day before in a shop at the nearby pier. While running a brush through her hair, she ran over the conversation she planned to have with Devon in the morning, causing nervous eruptions in her stomach.

Slipping into black sandals, Vic pulled her hair into a ponytail and fastened it with a stretch of black elastic as she hurried out the door.

"You can't turn me down, Devon," she muttered as she closed it behind her and she shook her head. "I'm not going to let you."

Chapter Ten

Drew and Louie were impatiently awaiting her arrival at the bottom of the stairs, and she felt compelled to offer a quick sorry before traipsing off alongside them.

It was her first time venturing out across the sand since her arrival in Florida, and she felt rather excited as she trudged her way toward the covered table where Penelope was waiting.

"Oh, you came!" she cried as the threesome approached. "I'm so glad."

Vic tried to ignore the grimace she saw Drew flash at Penelope out of the corner of her eye.

"I had to see what all the fuss was about," she said with a smile. Then, looking directly at Drew, she added, "I won't make a habit of it."

"Don't be silly," Penelope reassured her. "We're happy to have you."

Well, one of you, maybe. As Louie circled her, wagging his tail so hard that it looked like it might knock him over, she thought, *Okay, two of you.*

"Why don't you go get your feet wet while I spread out the fixins," Penelope offered. "Andrew, walk with her."

Looking for all the world like a child just sent to his room, Drew headed out across the sand.

"C'mon," he muttered to Vic as he passed.

"Such a pleasant invitation," she replied sarcastically, and then shot a smile in Penelope's direction, "how can a girl refuse?"

They reached the water's edge in silence, and Vic stepped out of her shoes and approached the waning surf. Cool bubbles of liquid foam floated over her feet, and she sighed as she tilted her head backward and looked up at the sky.

"It certainly is beautiful here," she remarked, but Drew didn't reply.

"So, who's Devon?" he finally asked after a few minutes of silence had inched past.

"A business associate," she answered softly, and Drew's attention darted toward her.

"I guess they miss you up there. Maybe he wants you to come home."

"I doubt that," she said.

"That he misses you? Or that he wants you back?"

"Both."

Vic had pinned such a large part of her plans for Romantic Overtures on the hope that *Tying the Knot* would come onboard with her ideas. If they didn't . . .

No! she stopped herself. *They will. They have to.*

But in the meantime, she was determined not to share her sinking sense of impending failure with Drew. He was the client, after all. And you never let anything on to the client.

Drew released a throaty sigh, and thankfully didn't inquire further.

"I'm sorry if I intruded on your outing with Penelope," she said after a few beats.

"You didn't."

"Oh. Well, you were acting like I did."

"No. You didn't."

Vic stared at Drew for a moment, but he didn't meet her gaze. His eyes remained fixed on something far away in the distance.

"Then what's your problem?"

He looked at her, and the intensity of it made her wish he hadn't.

"What do you mean?"

"Ever since I told you Penelope invited me to come along with the two of you, you've been acting like a schoolboy who didn't get his way at recess. What's up, Drew? If you don't want me hanging around, I can easily make my excuses and be on my way."

He lowered his eyes, and then sighed.

"I'm sorry. Just ignore me," he said softly.

"Have I done something to offend you?"

"No."

"Then cough it up, Nolan. What's your problem?"

Drew raised his eyes again and met her gaze with a disarming smile.

"Do you like chicken, or what?"

"Yes," Vic said with a chuckle. "I like chicken."

"Then let's go eat some."

Vic stood there for a moment, not sure whether to press the issue or simply allow him to brush it away.

"C'mon and put your shoes on," he said, reaching for her hand and taking it gently into his. "You've never tasted anything like this, I guarantee you."

Louie trotted on ahead of them as they plodded across the sand, and the warm feel of Drew's palm pressed against hers sent rays of warmth rippling up her arm.

Polite conversation ran the gamut—from the delicious chicken and mouth-watering cole slaw to the clouds rolling in on the horizon to obstruct the coming sunset. Vic offered a recap of her meeting with Tiffany and Sasha, and Drew filled her in on a completed project that would now free him up to help where needed with the wedding plans.

"You want to help with . . . the wedding?"

"Our Drew is adept at hiding it, but he does have quite a sentimental streak," Penelope defended.

"Does he?" Vic teased. "I hadn't noticed."

"Well, he doesn't expose it often. I'd guess there are a lot of hidden talents that would surprise you about Andrew."

"All right, ladies," Drew interjected, sweeping a napkin across his mouth and tossing it onto the table. "Quit talking about me like I'm not here, or you may get your wish."

"That's not my wish," Vic said spontaneously, and she was immediately sorry that she had.

"No?" he asked curiously.

"Well, no," she admitted. "I'm glad you're here."

Drew looked at her strangely for a moment, then smiled proudly.

Quickly handing over the stack of paper plates and used napkins that she'd gathered, she added, "We needed someone to do the clean-up."

Drew bent over in mock-injury, releasing a groan before taking the trash from her hands and walking it over to the metal barrel at the edge of the concrete slab beneath the picnic table.

"Okay, Miss Smarty Pants," he said as he sat down next to her on the wooden bench. "Penelope did the cooking, I did the clean-up. What, pray tell, is your contribution to the festivities?"

Vic thought it over seriously for a moment. Striking a fast and dramatic pose, she replied, "I'm prettying up the place."

Penelope let loose with a belt of laughter, and Drew followed suit with a chuckle of his own.

"Well, you'll get no argument from me on that," he said softly, and then looked away.

A flush of heat bolted through her, and Vic released the pose and folded her hands gently on the top of the table.

The wind had really begun to kick up, and Drew called out to Louie to summon him away from the water.

"Looks like our sunset is going to have to be re-scheduled," Penelope noted as she quickly began packing up the leftovers into the wicker basket she'd brought along.

"Why? What do you mean?" Vic asked disappointedly.

"Take a look at the sky," Drew said, pointing out a particularly ominous formation of black clouds hanging low over the choppy water. "Looks like we're in for a storm."

A gust of wind tossed its reckless agreement at them just then, and Drew reflexively reached out to stable Vic just before she lost balance from the impact.

"Whoa!" she cried. "Thank you."

"Do you have your car?" he asked Penelope, and she nodded confidently.

"Lucky thing," she said, observing the sky. "I might have been camping out at your place otherwise."

"Louie!" Drew called, smacking his leg emphatically, and then pulling Vic by the elbow. "Let's go, buddy."

A sudden jolt of lightning lit up the twilight sky, and the roaring clap of thunder that followed seemed to propel the dog toward his master.

"Do you want a ride back?" Penelope asked, struggling against the wind to fold the cotton tablecloth.

"Nope. We're on our way right now."

Vic waved helplessly at Penelope and shouted a thank-you into the wind as Drew pulled her along.

"Thanks for the meal," she sputtered. "It was terrific."

"Go!" Penelope said as she waved her arms. "Go!"

"Let's go," Drew commanded, and both he and Vic set out against the tempest toward home.

"This sure did roll in quickly," Vic noted as she pressed along behind him. "I've never seen such a thing."

"Tropical depression," Drew called out over his shoulder, and then paused to take her hand. "This is Florida weather for you."

Just as they reached the edge of the sand and Drew took his first step onto paved concrete, another strike of lightning lit the greenish-black sky behind them. A rolling peal of thunder followed, sending a sudden blitz of rain as its finale.

"Oh no!" Vic cried.

"We'd better run," Drew told her, instinctively wrapping his arm around her shoulder as they set out on a trot across the street. "C'mon, Lou!"

When they finally reached home, Drew guided Vic ahead of him up the stairs. Even through the solid curtain of rain, he couldn't fail to notice the alluring sway of her hips as she jogged up the steps just a few inches in front of him. Her light denim jeans had turned nearly black with moisture, and the fabric clung to her curves like second skin.

Louie looked very much like an oversized drowned rat when they reached the top of the stairs and found him waiting on the landing. Before he could direct the dog elsewhere, he flew into the apartment the moment Vic opened the door.

"No, Louie," he called. "Let's go home."

"Oh, it's all right," she told him. "Come on in. I'll grab some towels and make some coffee."

Drew wasn't entirely sure how great an idea this was, but he followed her inside and pressed hard against the wind to shut the door. When he turned back, Vic was already spreading a bright red towel over Louie's back and rubbing him hard to soak up the moisture. The dog turned his face toward her as if she were the goddess of all that was good in the universe, causing Drew to shake his head in dismay.

"Here," he said, taking over the task. "I'll do that. You get into some dry clothes."

"Here's one for you," she told him, tossing a second towel toward him before she headed down the hall.

When he pulled the towel from Louie's back, the dog shook a spray of what was left of the downpour in all directions, hitting Drew's face in particular.

"That's what I get, huh?" he commented, and the dog grinned unapologetically over his shoulder.

Drew unsnapped the buttons of his denim shirt and pulled the tails from the waistband of his Wranglers. Heading into the kitchen, he quickly put on a pot of coffee and produced two clean mugs from the cabinet.

"If you take off your shirt and your socks, I can toss them in the dryer for a little while," Vic suggested as she appeared behind him.

"Ah, no, thanks," he said. "I'll go on home in a few minutes and change."

"Well, at least take off your shoes and socks," she said on a chuckle. "You're sloshing all around in my kitchen."

Drew turned to face her and was taken back by what he saw. Her ebony hair was combed loosely away from her face, just one tiny lock hanging down into her crystal blue eyes. Her face glistened, scrubbed clean of any trace of make-up, just a tiny smattering of auburn freckles radiating out from her small nose, giving the impression that she had just been dusted with a wayward pinch of cinnamon. Her full lips were invitingly unadorned, blushed with the natural color of warm cherry preserves.

"What?" she asked him self-consciously, and it was at that moment that he realized, quite unabashedly, that he'd been staring at her.

"Coffee?" he asked with a raspy note of surprise.

"I'll pour. You go get out of those wet shoes."

Drew had just settled down onto the sofa and removed his shoes when a firebolt of lightning ignited the dim room through the windows, and the entire place plummeted into complete darkness immediately afterward.

"Drew?"

"Okay," he told her, rising to his feet. "Stay right where you are. I'll come to you."

"I've got two cups of hot coffee in my hands," she warned him. "And I can't see to set them down."

"Keep talking," he said, awkwardly making his way through the dark.

"Umm, okay," she replied obediently. "I think I'm about three steps outside of the kitchen . . . and it's pitch black in this place . . . and I guess the electricity is out, so we'd better find some candles or a flashlight or something . . . Gee, I'm glad we made coffee before the power went out because—Ouch!"

"Sorry," Drew said, drawing back from where he'd just stumbled directly into her. "Are you hurt?"

"No, a little coffee sloshed out on my hand," she said. "I'm okay."

"All right, I'm taking the cups from you right now," he instructed. "Now I'm turning back toward the dining room. You stay right where you are."

The corner of the table announced its presence to his hip and he carefully set the cups down on it. Blinking his eyes several times in an attempt to adjust to the darkness, he turned and noticed the slight silhouette of the ribbed white tanktop Vic was wearing. Although he couldn't see her, his memory quickly recalled the light gray sweatpants, tied in a little bow which was situated just beneath her belly button.

"I see you," he told her as he approached, and then he took her by the wrist. "That's you, right?"

"What do you mean? What's me?" she asked, and then giggled mischievously. "No, I'm kidding. It's me."

Drew grinned broadly in the dark. There were times like these when this pit bull, as he and Pen had taken to calling her, was almost too adorable to bear.

"Just follow me slowly," he said. "I'll lead you over to the couch."

"Okay. I'm following," she replied as she placed her hands on either side of his waist and followed so closely that he could feel the warmth of her flesh pressed against his back. "All aboard."

"Here we go. Come around this way. Be careful of the coffee table."

"Okay, I'm good. I've found it."

"Are you sitting?"

"No."

"Well, sit."

"Okay." And he heard her perfect round fanny as it plopped down on the couch. "Hey, you know, I bought some candles yesterday at the pier. They're in a bag in the hall closet."

"The hall closet," he repeated, making his way through the dark in the general direction of the closet.

Locating the bag was simple enough, and Drew used the wall to guide him back around to the dining room where he recalled seeing a cigarette lighter lying on the table. Only a few more moments passed before the room was illuminated with the flickering yellow light of several large pillar candles, each of them with three wicks of their own. One of them gave off the fragile fragrance of raspberries, and another was thickly scented with vanilla.

Drew moved toward the couch and sat down, setting the mugs on the coffee table in front of them.

"Does this happen often?" she asked, and he noticed a slight nervous lilt to her voice.

"The storms or the power outage?"

"Both."

"The storms come in seasons, and the bad ones knock down lines or produce surges," he explained calmly. "But there are people who know what they're doing, and they'll restore the power pretty quickly. It's nothing to worry about."

"Okay."

She didn't seem to stand entirely behind her agreement, but Drew sensed that she'd decided to take him at his word.

"If it doesn't come back on in a few minutes, I'll go over and get a radio that operates on batteries, and we'll see what they have to say about the storm," he offered. "Would that make you feel better?"

"Yes."

It dawned on him that tropical storms and the problems that came with them were probably about as foreign to Vic as a massive subway shutdown would be to him. Ever so often, he'd been able to forget that Victoria Townsend was an alien in his land, a castaway with no real comprehension about things like hurricanes and sunsets, palm trees and smoothies. And then a moment like this one would occur, and he was faced with the vivid reminder that her world and his were galaxies apart. Her planet was filled with taxi cabs and garbage strikes, traffic jams and cigarette smoke.

"Hey," he realized aloud. "Did you quit smoking? Again?"

She laughed out loud at his distinction, and the song of it jangled against his chest.

"Again?"

"Well. After setting your purse on fire."

She charmed him with her laughter one more time before replying, "I haven't had a smoke since then."

"I'm proud of you," he offered.

"Thank you. I'm sort of proud of me too. But it's a daily struggle. Hourly, when big things happen, like storms and power outages."

"This will pass," he reassured her. "And so will your cravings."

"I hope you're right."

The feeling between them was unusually comfortable, and Drew turned sideways on the couch, folding his legs beneath him as he faced her. Louie, having picked up on the casual environment, made a slow crawl up to the couch and turned in a complete circle before curling into a ball between them. He released a long, laborious sigh before closing his eyes.

"Can I ask you something?" Vic piped, then paused to take a long sip from her coffee.

"Sure. I'm not saying I'll answer. But you can ask."

"Why were you so strange with me down at the beach earlier.

Your whole mood changed when Penelope invited me to come along."

Drew winced slightly, then covered it by reaching for his own cup of coffee and indulging momentarily.

"Penelope is a very stubborn woman," he began cautiously. "And she has it in her head that it would be a good thing for you and I to . . . pursue . . . a . . . you know . . . personal scenario."

"Ohhh." He waited for further comment, but none followed.

"I've explained to her that we are business associates, and that anything further than that is not an option. But she has her own thoughts on the matter—and on most matters, now that I think of it—and she invited you to come along as a sort of cattle prod to get my butt in gear with you."

"And you resented that." She said it as a statement rather than an inquiry.

"Well, yes."

"I see."

"I enjoy spending time with you, don't get me wrong. But this is business between us."

"Right," she nodded slowly, deliberately.

"And my business is in deep trouble."

"Yes, it is."

"We need to be focused one hundred percent on getting to the bottom of the trouble, and making the necessary repairs. A personal scenario would only cloud that—"

"Most likely."

"—and divert us from the goals at hand."

"Right."

She didn't sound as resolved as he would have liked.

"Well, don't you agree?" he prodded.

"Of course."

Her eyes shimmered at him in the dark, reflecting the glow of candlelight against a silhouette so perfect and sweet that she could have been a face carved on the front of a cameo. He wanted to, but he couldn't look away from her. She was as fascinating to him as toys in a shop window when he was a kid, and he was drawn inside with just one look.

"Drew," she said suddenly, and the sound of it was nearly lost against the downpour of rain just outside.

"Yes?"

"I . . ."

They both jumped as the lights flickered twice and then rose to full power. Louie barked once and leapt to the floor while a pain shot through Drew at the sudden starkness of the room, and he shielded his eyes against the intrusion.

"I guess you were right," Vic said, and he watched her as she carried both of the coffee mugs into the kitchen, pausing to blow out the candles on the dining tabletop.

He was on his feet when she returned, and he made his way slowly toward the front door.

"It's time I get home then," he muttered.

"I wish I had an umbrella to offer you. It's still raining pretty hard."

"I'm just the next door down. I'm sure I'll be fine."

"Alright."

"Thanks for the coffee."

"Thanks for the candlelight," she returned with a smile.

"Well, good night then."

"Good night."

Chapter Eleven

Vic watched Drew run down the landing to his own door as something inside her chest thudded along with him. As she closed the door and flipped the lock, she said a silent prayer of thanks to God for His timing.

"Do you ever think about that kiss we shared in your car?" she had been just about to ask Drew when the lights had flickered on. "Because I do," she had wanted to say. "Your lips still burn my mouth when it crosses my mind, your fingertips still sear the flesh on my arms where you touched me that night. And every time I think I'll be able to forget it, put it out of my mind, it creeps up out of nowhere and burns me again."

Would she really have been able to get those words out of her mouth? *Probably not,* she acknowledged. But they were there at the surface, just the same. Bubbling and roiling and simmering, and making her nicotine cravings pale in comparison with the desire for one more Drew Nolan kiss.

Devon McKay fluttered across her mind as she pulled back the blanket and crawled into bed, and a stream of fears and imaginings about their pending conversation softly washed away thoughts of Drew's lips, at least for the moment.

"My business is in deep trouble," he had told her, and the remembrance of his words caused the stress in her stomach to churn once again. "We need to be focused one hundred percent on getting down to the bottom of the trouble, and making the necessary repairs."

But, without Devon McKay's cooperation, completing her strategic battle plan was going to be near impossible. Failure wasn't something Vic conceded to easily, it never had been. And failing Drew was a concept that appealed even less.

I'll call Devon first thing in the morning, she vowed as she rolled over onto her back and flopped onto the pillow. *And I'll charm him right out of his reasons for turning me down.*

If all else failed, she admitted only to the deepest recesses of her soul, she would not be above pleading with him in this instance. She'd hardly ever failed at anything in her life, at least when it came to business, and she wasn't about to start now. So if begging was what it would take to avoid seeing disappointment staring back at her from the eyes of Andrew Nolan, then that's what she would do.

Rolling over and wrapping her arms around her pillow, clutching it to her in place of the warm body she now realized she craved, Vic nestled in and prepared for a long and sleepless night. But the rhythm of the rain harmonized with the backbeat of rolling thunder making its way out into the ocean, and in no time at all she had drifted off.

"It would have been Sol who called if it was going to be a go," Vic told Krissy as she tapped the eraser of her pencil on the desk with the intensity of a battering ram. "When Devon McKay calls, it can only mean bad news. So I have to beat him to the punch. I'll call him right away and, before he even has a chance to turn me down, I'll just . . ."

Vic's attention was dragged away from the conversation as Tiffany entered the conference room, waving her arms and pointing animatedly at the telephone.

"Hang on, Krissy," she said, covering the receiver with her palm. "What are you trying to tell me, Tiffany?"

"Someone named Devon is on line two."

Vic could almost hear the screeching brakes of her heart. "Okay. Thank you."

"Sure."

"I have to go. I'll call you back."

Before her assistant could reply, Vic disconnected the line and replaced the phone on its cradle. Staring at it in horror, as if it might jump up and do a little dance across the desktop at any moment, she battled against the nearly overwhelming desire to hop to her feet and run straight across the street and into the ocean.

"Vic? Line two?" Tiffany called out from reception.

"Heard you. Hold your horses."

They might have been as different in appearance as night and day, but it occurred to Vic just then that Krissy and Tiffany were actually two of a kind.

She sucked in as deep a breath as she could hold, and then released it slowly and deliberately before picking up the telephone receiver and punching the incessantly flashing light with the eraser of her pencil.

"Victoria Townsend," she stated seriously. "Thank you for holding."

"Hello, Victoria. Devon McKay here."

The rich and resonant tone of his voice did something to her insides, the manifestation of which was the clean snap of the pencil she'd been holding.

"Well, hello Devon. How have you been?"

"Different day, same agenda," he stated confidently, and the well-rehearsed perfection of it made her want to scream. "But you! It seems you have much to tell, my dear."

He called her "my dear" as if he were a close friend, not someone who held all the cards to a poker game that meant everything at the moment.

"Florida, Vic? What in the world were you thinking?"

"I was thinking, hey, there's a nothing little business down in St. Petersburg that's slipping into oblivion. They say it's too far gone to be saved."

"And so you had to be the one to prove them wrong," he assessed, causing Vic to smile in spite of herself.

The fact that she'd been exiled against her will, sent there kicking and screaming the whole way, and had to be blackmailed into actually getting on the plane . . . Well, these were facts not worth mentioning.

"You know how I love a challenge," she commented. "But to make a tediously long story as short as possible, one thing led to another, and this little wedding idea became the basis for a whole new business face. I'm very excited about it, Devon. It's going to be huge. I'm especially excited that I can count on you for help in promoting it."

"Vic," he sighed; the latent disappointment held within that sigh was so familiar to her that she felt her hope drop dramatically. "This is so beneath you."

"Look, it's a personal favor for an old friend of Trenton's," she said, trying a different track. "When I pull this off, I'll be adding the title of Creative Director to my Marchant Media business cards. You know how hard I've worked for that."

"I'm starting to see the light."

"Devon, you know me. You know I don't jump on a bandwagon that I can't get up to speed."

"I'm sorry, Vic," he said with a lilt that was only slightly patronizing.

"No, no," she warned him as she interrupted. "I don't want to hear your apologies, Devon. I want to hear your enthusiasm. What do I have to do to rev up your enthusiasm? Because, I'm telling you, this is something you don't want to miss out on."

"Just the same, this is a nothing business in the middle of nowhere that—"

"Look," she interrupted again. "Do this for me. Let me put together a little trailer for you, show you what we're looking at here. I'll have it sitting in your inbox in 72 hours, and I'm betting you'll see it differently. This is a very commercial concept."

"Oh, Vic," he replied with another sigh.

"Do this for me, Devon. I'm asking you as a personal favor."

"I'll tell you what I'm going to do for you," he said, and she rolled her eyes because she knew him far too well for her own good. "You get something to me in *forty-eight* hours, and we'll talk again. But if the hook isn't there—"

"It will be there, Devon. You'll have it before noon on Thursday."

"That's all I can give you, darlin'."

"For the moment, it's all I'm askin', sweet pea."

Devon's familiar chuckle sent a stream of hope cascading through every part of her body.

"I'll speak with you on Thursday."

Vic set the phone gently into the cradle before she released a spout of anxiety that came out as a full-fledged scream.

Vic hadn't completed the three-rap knock at Sasha's door when it flew open. Sasha looked as if she'd been struck by lightning, and at first Vic was a little concerned.

"Come in, come in, you two!" the designer exclaimed, ushering Vic and Tiffany inside with a nearly overwhelming flourish. "I could hardly wait for you to get here!"

The bed was rumpled, but had obviously not been utilized much, not for sleeping anyway, and a pot of coffee on the table was surrounded by a well-used cup and half a dozen empty sugar packets. Assorted sketch pads were strewn around the abandoned chair and several pencils lounged carelessly nearby.

"You!" Sasha cried, placing both hands on Tiffany's face and patting her cheeks gently. "You've inspired me!"

"I have?"

Vic grinned from ear to ear. She didn't think she'd ever seen Sasha in such a state.

"I could waste a lot of time showing you some of the different things I came up with for your wedding dress," she beamed. "But you know what? Let's just cut to the chase. I stumbled upon a stroke of brilliance at around four o'clock this morning."

Tiffany looked at Vic cautiously before smiling politely at Sasha. "All rightie then. Let's have a look-see."

Sasha twisted her long hair around her fist and then tossed it loosely over her shoulder before sucking in a deep breath. "Okay. If you don't like it, you're certainly welcome to be honest. After all, this is your wedding dress, and we want it to be exactly perfect. Everything you've dreamed of. But I'm fairly sure you're going to like what you see. I mean, I kept going over and over everything you said, and then it was like a sudden flash of light—"

"Sasha!" Vic interrupted. "For goodness sake, let's take a look!"

"Okay."

Another deep breath, and she picked up one of the sketch pads and set it out on the table before Tiffany. She turned back the cover as if she were revealing a glimpse into the most private places of her very soul.

Tiffany eyed the sketch carefully, and Vic stepped up behind her chair to have a look for herself.

The page was divided into two sections, showing both the front and back views of Sasha's creation. The top of the dress was a simple band of gathered white fabric, just a square really, held together by crisscrosses of rhinestones that formed a lace-up effect over a completely bare back. The midriff was bare as well, except for a scallop formed by a chain of little rhinestone W's that looped together at a belly button ring peeking out above a tight sarong-type skirt knotted low on one hip. The hem of the skirt was short beneath the knot, showing a good bit of long, slender leg, and it dipped diagonally to the longest point just above the knee of the opposite leg.

Oh my.

Vic had no words except those, and she didn't dare speak them out loud for fear of deflating Sasha's expanding bubble of enthusiasm.

"Now we could use any kind of fabric you choose," Sasha gushed nervously. "But my choice would be a silk organza, or maybe satin, to compliment the cut of the skirt. The rhinestone straps and belly chain could be clear stones, or if you wanted to add some color we could have something made in a soft pastel stone, or a bolder shade like sapphire blue or ruby red."

She waited, but Tiffany didn't utter a word. Her eyes were wide, glued to the page in what Vic interpreted to be sheer horror.

"Oh!" Sasha gasped, producing a second sketch pad bearing a simple drawing of woman's foot. "You said you wanted to be barefoot, so I was thinking we might adorn your feet with something like this." A chain of W's formed an ankle bracelet loop which extended across the top of the foot and connected at a ring around the center toe.

Sasha's soul-stirring excitement met Tiffany's silence in the air above them, and it made Vic want to cringe. At any moment, the designer's hopes were going to be dashed, and the momentum would be—

Vic jumped as Tiffany suddenly slumped against the table, dropped her head into her folded arms, and began to wail.

"There's nothing written in stone," Vic tried to calm her, gently stroking the back of her head. "These are just ideas. If you don't like them, we'll find something else."

Vic looked up and all but crashed into the disappointment evident in Sasha's misty eyes.

"We have plenty of time yet," Vic said trying to soothe them both over the rumble of Tiffany's sobs. "We'll find just the right thing, I promise you."

"No, no, no," Tiffany sniffled. "You don't understand."

"Then just tell me," Sasha said, falling into the opposite chair and scooting it closer. "Help me understand. I want to make this right for you."

Tiffany lifted her head to look at her, blackened streams of tears and eyeliner cascading down her face. She began to shake her head dramatically as she darted her gaze to Vic, and then back to Sasha.

"No," she cried insistently. "That's just it. This *is* right."

"What?" Vic and Sasha asked in unison.

"You took everything that was up here," she said, pulling at tufts of hair on either side of her head, "and you put it right there on the page."

"You . . . like it then?" Vic asked incredulously.

"Like it? Are you kidding? I love it! It's the most perfect wedding dress *EVER!*"

Tiffany and Sasha flew to their feet and collided in midair. The twosome hopped up and down, still wrapped in a mutual embrace, and Tiffany initiated a euphoric mantra about Sasha's utter brilliance while Vic slid down into her vacant chair and released a sigh.

"Oh, thank you, thank you, thank you," Tiffany suddenly cried, almost landing in Vic's lap as she hugged her enthusiastically. "Thank you, thank you, thank you!"

Tiffany's exuberance was beginning to give Vic a bit of a headache. The drive back to the beach from Sasha's hotel was only fifteen minutes, but the smile she'd pasted to her face in response to Tiffany's chatter was starting to throb, and she was relieved when they pulled into the empty parking lot in the front of the building.

"Well, I'm glad Sasha came up with something that made you so happy," Vic said as she started inside.

"I almost wish I could go back to New York with her," Tiffany beamed. "I'd love to be in on every stitch!"

"You have a lot of other plans to make right here," she commented.

When Tiffany started into the office after her, Vic added, "I didn't mean right now."

"I told Drew I'd help him out in the office today," she explained with a chuckle. "I don't have classes today."

"Oh. Alright."

Vic headed into the conference room and left Tiffany in the reception area to sort through the mail. The momentary silence was somewhat soothing, and she leaned back against the chair and closed her eyes. She had to get to work on selling Devon!

Vic plugged her digital camera into her laptop and was just about to start looking through the photos she'd shot at Sasha's hotel when—

"No way!" Tiffany exclaimed from the other room, and then a moment later the girl was standing in the doorway, a serious frown distorting her face and an unfolded document in her hand.

"What?"

"No wonder Drew's been looking like he's carrying the weight of the whole world these last few weeks."

"What do you mean?" Vic straightened, trying to focus in on the paperwork. All she could make out was the envelope, where an intricate sketch of a detailed floor plan had been doodled across the back with a sharp-tipped pencil.

"I can't believe he'd risk his family home, though."

Irritation bristled just behind her eyes, and Vic repeated, "What are you talking about?"

"This," Tiffany said, dropping the documents on the desk in front of her. "Drew took out a business loan to get this place up and running again. And he used the Nolan estate as collateral!"

Vic looked more closely at the legal agreement before her.

So that's it. She'd just assumed the recent padding of his business account had come from an inheritance of some kind.

"He's gambling all he has left on this business," Tiffany summarized, shaking her head at Vic. "I sure hope you're as good as he's betting that you are. Or he's going to lose everything."

Something plopped down into the pit of her stomach as Vic acknowledged her own similar hope.

"What's this?" she asked Tiffany, pointing out the sketch on the back of the envelope.

"Another one of those houses Drew's always drawing," she replied. "When I doodle, I draw trees and flowers. When Drew does, he plans houses and office buildings. I swear, sometimes—"

They both jolted suddenly when the front door opened and then slammed shut. Tiffany cringed, then scrambled to grab the papers from Vic, folding them quickly and tucking them back into the empty envelope still in her hand.

Louie scampered around the corner and lunged at Vic, knocking her back against the chair as he bathed her face in sloppy, wet kisses of joyful salutation.

"Put those away," Vic said with a whisper, and then set about the task of freeing herself from the dog's affections as Tiffany disappeared obediently around the corner.

"Lou! Get down!"

He reluctantly complied, circling Drew as he appeared in the doorway.

"What ever happened to the days when he'd just bark and growl at me to say hello?" Vic asked with a nervous giggle.

Drew smiled at her, then straddled a chair on the opposite side of the conference table.

"So how did it go with your designer friend?"

Tiffany didn't give her the chance to reply before joining them. She settled on the edge of the table and chattered on about every detail of the dress, from the little W-shaped rhinestones of the belly chain to the white magnolia she planned to pin into her hair.

"No more wisteria then?" he asked as if he were interested, then shot a grin at Vic. "What about the whole W-theme?"

"The wisteria is for my bouquet. But I want a magnolia in my hair instead of wearing some old traditional veil or something. And it will be *white*," she emphasized dramatically. "That's still a W. *White*. Don't you think it will be beautiful?"

"Yes," he said with a shrug. "I'm sure it *will*."

Tiffany giggled at his play on words before continuing on her course of describing the ankle ornaments, the fabric, the way the skirt would tie in a knot at her hip.

Vic watched Drew carefully as Tiffany prattled on, and the reality that he had taken such a huge risk on results she hadn't been able to guarantee set acid churning at the pit of her stomach again.

She hadn't realized the stakes were quite so high for him when she'd begun, but Vic was energized with new resolve at the revelation. This was more than just an assignment to fill the time until she could step into the coveted position of Creative Director. For Drew, this was life or death.

"Don't you think so, Vic?"

"Huh? I'm sorry. What did you say?"

"Where were you?" Drew asked her casually. "On another planet?"

"Oh. No, I was right here on this one," she told him truthfully. "Now, both of you, get out of here. I have work to do, and I'm on a deadline."

Chapter Twelve

The muscle spasm in Vic's back had taken on a rhythm all its own, and her neck had stiffened to the point that she wasn't sure she could get up out of the chair. She'd been at it for ten hours already, and there was still a ways to go, but she was long overdue for the break her entire body was screaming for.

"Ohhhhh," she groaned as she slowly stood up.

The pain between her shoulder blades nearly snatched the breath right out of her. She grabbed hold of the back of the chair as she balanced on one leg, turning the ankle of the other and cringing as it cracked its noisy dispute.

The sun was rising over the Gulf in the distance beyond her apartment window, and she squinted against the announcement. Wishing for a cigarette and a huge latte from the shop just a block down from her New York brownstone, Vic made her way into the kitchen and filled the kettle with water and clanked it to the stovetop. All-nighters had been a part of her routine back in the city, but so had caffeine and nicotine pick-me-ups. She wondered as she dropped the herbal tea bag into a mug how much good it would honestly do her.

Glancing into the dining room, Vic shook her head at the mess that was now her workplace. She'd pulled several photos of Tiffany's meeting with Sasha off her digital camera and then overlaid neon graphics to the preliminary sketches of the bride's—using the word loosely—gown. She'd added some animation and some titles, but it still wasn't enough. Working from the unedited videotape of Walter and Tiffany's engagement party at The Beachside Hut, she felt certain she'd be able to find something more. She had to put together something extraordinary for Devon McKay.

A fresh mug of orange spice tea firmly in her grasp, Vic returned to her computer and plugged in the video feed. The tape was cued up to the middle; pushing the play button, she was greeted instantly by footage of herself gathered into Drew's arms. She leaned back in her chair and sighed at the memory,

111

then took a sip of hot tea as he swirled her across the screen to the familiar tropical beat. How lovely it had been to dance with Drew that night! How natural it had felt to sink into the strength of his arms and allow him to lead her across the dance floor.

And then later, in the car, out front.

The warmth of the spicy tea cooled in comparison to the mere recollection of his lips planted against hers. As she closed her eyes momentarily, she could almost feel the scalding brush of his hand on her bare shoulder.

Vic shook loose the memory from her head, punctuating the decision with one hard punch at the stop button. This was no time to get lost in useless fantasies about Drew Nolan's kisses, or caresses, or dreamy eyes. She tapped at the rewind button, determined to use her time wisely by jotting down a few notes about what she should be looking for.

That toast offered by the best man was powerful, she forced herself to recall. Walter had referred to Tiffany as his dancing shoes, and the memory made Vic smile.

"The wind beneath his wingtips," she said aloud as the tape clunked to a stop.

Vic played through the rough cut for the second time, then fell back against the chair. It was good. But it wasn't great. The content was fine, but it wasn't quite sharp enough. Something was still missing.

She picked up the cordless and dialed.

"Tiffany, I need your help. Do you have some free time this afternoon?"

Twenty minutes hadn't passed before the platinum-haired angel landed at her door.

"What's up?" She grinned at Vic as she opened the door.

"You're studying graphic arts, aren't you?"

"And web design."

"Are you any good?"

Tiffany arched one pierced brow and stared at Vic as if the question were the most absurd she'd ever heard. Vic burst into laughter; if she had stopped to consider the source, she'd have known it was more out of relief than amusement.

"Help," Vic pleaded, pointing her toward the computer. "It needs something."

Tiffany clunked toward the cluttered dining room table in four-inch mules. Standing over the computer, she twirled the ring that hung low from her exposed belly button as Vic pressed the button to replay her creation.

"I haven't set it to music yet," Vic explained as the visuals drew them both in. "But I need a creative eye."

A crooked grin crept across Tiffany's face as she watched.

"What is this?" she finally asked, captivated by the screen before her.

"Watch it all the way through, and then I'll explain."

Vic plopped down in the chair in front of the computer as the production came to a close. After a moment of silence, she looked up at Tiffany hopefully.

"Well? What do you think?"

"What's it for?"

"Have you ever seen a show called *Tying the Knot?*" she asked, hitting the rewind button before spinning in her chair and facing Tiffany.

"Of course."

"I want them to do a segment on your wedding."

"Are you kidding me?" Tiffany looked at Vic intently, slowly lowering herself to the adjacent chair without even glancing behind her. Vic couldn't help thinking it was a good thing the chair was in place or her companion might have ended up in a heap on the floor.

"If I can make this wedding as compelling to the production staff at *Knot* as it is to me, and they produce a segment that airs on a national level, Romantic Overtures will be the next big thing."

"That's a great idea," Tiffany commented in a manner far more subdued than Vic had anticipated. "Drew must be beside himself."

"Well," Vic began, then paused, quickly trying to figure out the best way to solicit Tiffany's help without giving away too much about the opposition she'd faced from Devon McKay.

"You haven't told him? He's got a lot riding on this. You should tell him."

"I don't want to get his hopes up," she explained, fighting against the deflated feeling that periodically pressed in at the notion that she might fail. "My contact over at *Knot* is resisting, and I have less than twenty-four hours left to produce something so compelling that they'll fall all over themselves to jump onboard."

"But Drew is very creative, Vic. You're not giving him credit for—"

"Drew also has a lot to lose here," she interrupted. "You saw those mortgage papers. And in my experience, nothing dampens the creativity in a person better than desperation."

And one desperate person on this project is more than enough!

"Can you help me?"

Tiffany didn't reply for what seemed like an eternity. Vic was just about to give in to the fear that was winding its way around her heart when—

"Let's watch it one more time," Tiffany suggested as she tore off her denim jacket and moved in toward the computer screen.

Vic couldn't help the smile that quickly spread across her face. The two of them couldn't possibly have been more different in every way, but the intensity in the girl's eyes, the metaphoric rolling up of the sleeves and getting down to business . . . That kind of focus was a universal language to Vic, and she recognized it right off because it was her own native tongue.

"Tying the Knot is a streamlined production," Tiffany commented resolutely. "They produce segments with edge, a little bit of bite to them."

Something inside Vic began to soar. Never in her wildest dreams could she have imagined finding a kindred spirit in the likes of Tiffany! But find her, she had. And relief began to flow through every throbbing artery of ambition and drive inside her.

"You know what would work here?" Tiffany continued enthusiastically. "Splashes of animation and color. And we could bring those titles up on a tilt, and have them fade back into this frame right here . . ."

Thank you, God.

"Now, the music is going to be important. They use a lot of kitch in their segments, you know? What about Billy Idol?"

Vic laughed out loud as Tiffany belted out the song.

"It's a . . . nice day for a . . . white wedding."

Vic joined her at the top of her lungs on the next line of the song. *"It's a . . . nice day to . . . start agaaaaaain . . ."*

"My God, we're geniuses!" Tiffany had exclaimed when they'd viewed the final version for the second time. "We are freakin' brilliant!"

Vic wasn't sure if the assessment stemmed from exhaustion after having spent another four hours on the task, but she was inclined to agree with the declaration. They'd produced an edgy five minutes of visual salesmanship at its finest, and Tiffany's surges of creativity and originality had only served to fuel the fire of Vic's own inspiration. Tiffany had sacrificed her morning classes for the cause, and they'd worked together more effectively than any creative team Vic had ever been a part of. The finished product was professional and polished and, best of all, it was something Vic felt confident would snatch her the brass ring.

To Devon McKay, from Victoria Townsend. Subject: Romantic Overtures.

The note attached to the download was short and sweet.

Devon, I hope you have a fresh pair of socks in your desk drawer because you're about to have your current ones knocked right off your feet. Vic.

She hit the send button before releasing the breath she'd been holding, then spent the next couple of minutes staring at the computer screen before her. There was nothing to do now but wait.

And pray.

Please, God . . .

The growling of her stomach reminded Vic suddenly just

how long it had been since she'd eaten. Or seen the light of day, for that matter.

Glancing out the window, she realized there wasn't much light to accompany the day. A storm looked to be rolling in, and she wanted to get out for a quick bite before it did.

After a fast shower, she jumped into her favorite black sweat pants and zipped up a hooded jacket on her way out the door. For some reason, the Gulf seemed to be calling to her on that particular afternoon. She stopped at the lunch stand across the alley for a chicken caesar to go and carted it off toward the water.

She chose the same picnic table she'd shared with Penelope and Drew on another afternoon when a similar storm was gathering above them. The sun tried to poke through for no more than a moment before dark clouds got the better of it, and a slight mist whispered down into the crash of waves at the shoreline.

Vic headed back across the sand a half hour later to find Drew wrestling with some folded cardboard boxes that didn't seem to want any part of being shoved into the back seat of his convertible.

"Moving day?" she teased as she approached and Louie greeted her with joyous barks of exhilaration.

"I've got some things to pack up out at the house," he replied.

"Can I tag along?"

Drew looked at her curiously for a moment before nodding with a shrug. "If you want."

"If I don't get a change of scenery today, I might just crack up entirely."

"What, again?" he teased, and Vic laughed out loud as she rounded the car and slipped inside.

Louie leapt over the driver's seat and into the back, skittering across the layer of cardboard boxes until he found a few inches to call his own. Drew dropped behind the wheel and shot Vic a smile.

"So what have you and Tiffany been up to?" he asked as he backed out and headed for the road. "You've been holed up in your apartment for two days. When I saw her come out of there today she looked like she'd been through the war."

"She was helping me put together a promo," Vic replied casually. "She's actually pretty gifted."

"What kind of promo?"

"Just something to garner some interest. Nothing set in stone as yet."

She felt a gust of relief at the center of her chest as Drew appeared to change gears.

"I took a call this morning from a guy who works with Walter Weems," he told her. "I met him and his girlfriend at the engagement party."

"Oh?"

"Yeah, he's interested in coming in and talking about our services. He's getting ready to propose and Walter told him we'd take care of everything, make it something special."

"Drew, that's great!" she exclaimed, patting his hand with hers several times. "Things are falling right into place."

"He's coming in on Friday. You'll be around, right?"

"Of course. But you could handle it on your own."

Drew let out a single-syllable chuckle and then shook his head.

"I don't know," he said, turning off the main road and down a narrow tree-lined street. "It got me to thinking about what I'm going to do when your business here is done and I have to fly solo through this sort of thing."

"You'll do great," she said assuredly.

"I'm no wedding planner, Vic."

"You'll get the hang of it. And if all goes as planned, you'll be able to afford to hire some professional help along the way."

"Still . . ." he began, then fell silent.

Vic watched him for a long moment, noting the intensity in his narrowed eyes.

"You won't be picking the flowers and putting together the bouquets yourself. This is going to be big business. You'll just be overseeing it. And I won't turn you loose on any unsuspecting couples until you have the help you need to do it right."

He seemed to be mulling that over, then nodded slightly.

"Don't worry, Drew. It's going to be fine."

He glanced at her questioningly, then smiled. "If you say so."

"I do. I say so."

"Alright then."

One more turn down a remote road, and there it was before them. So this was the family home Drew had risked to save the life of his business!

"Drew, it's beautiful!" she declared as the car rolled to a stop out front.

"It needs a lot of work," he replied. "I'm ashamed to say I've neglected it a little over the last year or so."

As the convertible top slowly cranked back into place, Louie galloped over the boxes and hopped through the open door, landing on the ground with a thud before Drew could unload them to afford an easier exit.

Vic meandered around the side of the house and absorbed the expanse of land that surrounded it.

"Is this where you grew up?" she asked Drew as he joined her.

"This is it."

"Wow."

"Oh, come on," he chuckled, then took her arm and led her back toward the front of the house. "Trenton didn't raise you in some warehouse somewhere."

"No," she acknowledged as she followed him. "But we always lived in the city. I wouldn't have known what to do with this kind of wide open space unless it was called Central Park."

Drew laughed at that, and Vic followed him up the wooden stairs, through the front door and into the foyer.

"Drew, this house!"

"Yeah, it's pretty special," he said as he headed through the hall to the kitchen. "It was a two thousand, nine hundred and forty square foot labor of love for my dad."

Enormous windows overlooked a deck that led to a back yard that seemed to go on for miles.

"He had it built?"

"Designed it, contracted it, and worked right alongside the builders from the foundation to the shingles."

"Really?"

"Four bedrooms, two baths, a great room, a formal dining room, den, atrium and mud room."

"An atrium," she considered thoughtfully.

"My mom loved plants."

"I kill them like clockwork. Thirty days, almost to the minute, and they're goners, no matter what the species."

"I'll keep that in mind."

Drew dropped the cardboard boxes on the center island, and Vic meandered behind him as he headed through the arched entry to the great room, and on into the den. Leaded glass broke prism-like patterns in what was left of the sunlight streaming through the windows, and two of the four walls housed sturdy floor-to-ceiling bookcases beneath arches of intricately carved molding.

Drew opened the huge roll-top desk near the window with the turn of an ornate brass key, then began rifling through dozens upon dozens of rolled tubes of paper held in place by colorful rubber bands.

Sidestepping to the window, Vic traced the path of the Southern-style porch that wrapped its way around the perimeter of the house. It brought about visions of lazy summer afternoons, sipping lemonade and reading one of the hundreds of novels packed tightly into the shelves surrounding her.

"Hold out your arms."

She did as she was told, and Drew began dropping the paper tubes he pulled from the desk into her arms.

"What are these?"

"Blueprints and floor plans," he stated without further explanation.

"Floor plans for what?" Vic finally asked.

"Houses, mostly."

"What are they for?"

"Dreaming. I've been collecting them for years."

"Why are you packing them up?" she inquired despite his demeanor, which spoke sternly of his unwillingness to explain.

"Organization, I guess," he admitted. "I want to have them all in one place."

"Oh."

She'd responded as if she understood, but Vic clearly did not. Where were the others? she wanted to ask. And why did he collect them to begin with? People collected things like stamps or dolls or spoons, or even matchbook covers like Krissy. She'd never heard of anyone collecting blueprints!

Beyond the window, Vic noticed the sky had turned a menacing shade of dark green, and the rain that had threatened her at the beach earlier in the day was now rolling in with purpose. The trees outside were dipping in the wind, and the leaves seemed to be turned inside out as the downpour began.

"Great," Drew commented, snatching up the last armload himself. "I'd hoped to get back to the office before it began."

A clap of thunder propelled Louie into the den where he curled up at Drew's feet. As Drew headed out of the room and back toward the kitchen, Vic and Louie followed him silently.

Just as she reached the doorway, a simple misstep caused one of the tubes in her arms to smack lightly against the jamb. It was like an unfortunate game of Dominoes to Vic as the blueprints began to tumble, one after the other, over her arms and across the floor.

"Oh, phooey!"

The clamor didn't seem to phase Drew in the least, and he remained in the kitchen a full couple of minutes before she was able to gather her wits, as well as her baggage, and meet up with him at the kitchen table.

There was something about the resolve with which he was packing up the cardboard box with belongings, and it occurred to Vic that perhaps Drew had lost hope in saving his family home.

"You're not giving up, are you?" she asked him timidly as she began unloading her own batch of paper tubes into one of the empty boxes.

"On what?"

She wasn't supposed to know about the second mortgage on the house, but it seemed to her like Drew had already counted it lost.

"I don't know, really," she said. "You just seem very resigned today. Is something troubling you?"

"I guess I always get like this when I come back to this house," he answered softly. "A lot of memories here."

"Oh."

Once again, if it appeared that Vic understood, she supposed appearances would be gravely mistaken.

Chapter Thirteen

"Drew, you'll never believe it! You'll never believe what's happened!" Vic cried between kisses, and Drew circled her waist with his arms, lifting her off the ground.

"Whatever it is," he said with a burst of laughter, "it looks to be all good."

"Oh, I'm sorry," she chuckled, untangling herself from him and stepping back down to the ground. "I'm just so excited. Come on in and let me tell you all about it."

Drew followed her inside and closed the door after Louie had snuck inside as well.

"It's just so unbelievable," she began. "Remember Devon McKay called me the other day?"

"The guy from New York who probably didn't want you to come back."

Oh, great, he thought. *Here it comes. 'We used to date and now he's realized he can't live without me. I'm going home on the next plane.'*

"Right!" she nodded, tugging him by the hand toward the dining room table. "Well, he's the associate producer for *Tying the Knot.* Do you know that show?"

"No."

"I pitched him a segment on Tiffany's wedding because, if we're going to go national with your company, *Tying the Knot* is the top entry on the wish list."

"He's a business contact then." Relief pounded in the pit of his stomach.

"Well, if they were going to do it, Sol would have been the one to call. When Devon calls, it's always bad news. Always, every time."

"Oh." *So what are you saying then?*

"Every time, except this one!" she cried joyously. "Tiffany and I put together a five minute spot for him, something to try and sell him on the idea, and he loved it. Loved it! He wants everything we've got so far, and they're sending a camera crew down to interview Walter and Tiffany, to profile the business, and to shoot the wedding! Can you believe it?"

"No," he admitted. "That's . . . uh . . ." *What? What is it??* ". . . . great."

"Oh, it's far more than great!" she told him. "It's a miracle!"

Wrapping her arms around his neck one more time, Vic hugged him and planted an enthusiastic kiss on the center of his cheek.

"We should go out and celebrate," he suggested carefully. "We have a lot to talk about."

"That's a great idea! I'll call Tiffany and invite her and Walter along so I can prep them. And maybe they can give us the lowdown on how to prepare for Walter's friend. Isn't he coming in tomorrow? We've got a lot of work to do, Drew."

Not exactly the evening I had in mind, he thought forlornly.

The waitress set a heaping platter of mussels before them, the edible inside peeking out of the half-opened shells through a glaze of garlic and wine.

Raising his glass of chardonnay toward the center of the table, Walter offered a toast to the future success of Romantic Overtures, and their four glasses clinked out an agreement.

"And to the future Mr. and Mrs. Weems," Vic added happily. "Without whom, this might not be possible."

"I'm so happy for you, Drew," Tiffany told him. "This is just what you wanted."

"Yeah," he nodded. "Thank you."

Vic wondered at his lackluster smile, but decided to dismiss it for the time being. Everything about Drew had been strangely subdued lately, and she attributed it to his general stress over the business. He would see soon enough how much of a shining difference this new victory was going to mean for him, and she hoped for a corresponding change of spirit.

"It was such a rush," Tiffany was telling Walter when Vic turned into the conversation again. "Like a creative shot of adrenaline, right in the chest! Working with Vic was so exciting."

"Well, you are largely responsible for Devon agreeing to do

the segment. You did a great job," Vic told her truthfully. "You're very talented."

"I can hardly wait to go out there and get a job doing something like that," Tiffany remarked. "If things go really well for you after this spot, do you think I might be able to get a job with you after graduation, Drew?"

"When do you graduate?" Vic cut in.

"The end of this semester," she replied. "And I'm getting married in two weeks! I'm all grown up."

"Bite your tongue," Walter interjected as Tiffany leaned in coyly and accepted his kiss.

"Working with Drew wouldn't really be what you've studied for," Vic pointed out. "It's not all video production and computer work."

"Oh, I know. I just love the idea of being around weddings all the time, and couples in love. Helping them plan their big events, and seeing their faces when everything goes just the way they hope it will. Like the day I met Sasha!"

"So when am I going to see this secret wedding attire you've chosen for us?" Walter asked, looking from one of them to the other.

"On our wedding day," Tiffany answered stubbornly.

"What, you'll just bring me a garment bag and tell me to put on whatever is inside?"

"Something like that. Do you mind?"

"Not in the least," he conceded softly. "As long as it made you happy, I'd wear a tomato costume and play the tuba."

"Don't be silly," Tiffany returned. "You know you don't look good in red."

The three of them laughed at that, and Vic noticed Drew making an effort to join in. But his heart wasn't in it, of that she was certain.

The drive home was more of the same. He was pleasant enough, making conversation and smiling in all the right spots, but the downcast haze of his eyes wouldn't let go of Vic's heart.

"Drew?"

"Yeah," he replied, his arm sloped casually over the steering wheel.

"Do you trust me?"

He glanced over at her curiously for a moment, and then looked back at the road. "Yes. Of course, I do."

"Then please talk to me."

"What do you want to discuss?"

"I think you know. What's bothering you?"

Drew was quiet for several minutes. From the look of him, someone wouldn't even have known he'd been involved in a conversation of any kind. And just about the time that Vic was about to stir up the exchange one more time, he suddenly pumped at the brake and pulled the car slowly over to the side of the road and shut off the key.

There was nothing on either side of them except wooded patches of muddy grass, and long strands of peat moss hung from the tree branches like tinsel from a Christmas tree. The road was completely barren aside from their car, and the silence of the night was disguised beneath the incessant croaks and chirps of the Florida wild.

Drew turned sideways in the driver's seat and faced Vic seriously.

"I can see there's something nagging at you," she offered. "And I'd really like to help, if I can. Or just listen, if you need someone to talk to."

"Don't you ever get tired of trying to solve the problems of other people?" he asked her with a weary, crooked smile.

"Yes," she said honestly. "Sometimes."

"Then why don't you stop? You don't always have to know what's churning around inside another person, do you?"

"No," she conceded. "Not always."

"But in this case?"

"In this case, I do."

One side of Drew's mouth curled upward in an inept attempt at a smile which Vic returned with a full-fledged grin of her own.

"You think you'll feel better if you know what's on my mind?" he asked her.

"I don't know. But it can't be much worse than wondering."

"Even if it turns out to be you that's bothering me?"

Her heart rattled once before continuing on to the next beat in the line. "I'm bothering you?" she asked carefully.

"Very much."

"Can you expound a little for me?"

"If you think it will help."

"Definitely," she urged him. "I'd like to know."

A thousand things hopped about simultaneously inside her head. If she were frank, Vic would have to admit that she did tend to get on the bad side of people every now and then. More often than not, she realized, it was a result of her approach to business, and she wondered if she'd inadvertently waltzed over Drew's pride one more time without being aware of it.

"Oh," she muttered as the recollection started to dawn. "This is about Tiffany, isn't it? She asked about a job and I didn't let you handle it. I'm sorry, Drew. I didn't mean to jump ahead, but you know she really would be an asset to you as things progress and—"

"No," he stopped her, placing two fingers gently over her lips. "It's not about Tiffany."

"It's not?" she garbled past his fingers.

"No. It's not." His fingers slipped gently from her mouth, and his hand came to rest on the slope of her shoulder.

"Then what is it? Something related to my big mouth, no doubt."

"Yes. It is related to your mouth."

What did I say this time?

"In direct relation to your mouth, as a matter of fact," he told her in earnest.

"Well, what is it?"

"I want to kiss it."

"I beg your pardon?"

"I spend a great deal of time thinking about your mouth, Victoria. And your eyes. And—"

"What?"

"—your legs."

"Drew—"

"I'm attracted to you, Vic. And I find that fact extremely—"

"I thought we covered this already. You're a client, and we can't—"

"—disturbing."

"—get involved in a romantic way. What do you mean, disturbing?"

Drew's hand slid around to the back of her neck where he squeezed her gently before removing his touch completely.

"I don't want to be attracted to you," he explained. "You're all wrong for me."

"Well . . . you're all wrong for me, too," she said, noting the defensiveness that had slipped into her tone.

"But knowing that doesn't seem to change anything," he explained, turning to face forward. "And when I think about you packing up and going back to New York in a few months, I feel . . . a lot like the bottom is dropping out of my life."

"You do?"

"Yes," he said as he turned back to face her again. "I do."

Vic took a deep breath, then massaged it past the lump in her throat.

"I guess what I want to know is . . . Do you ever think about me? You know, romantically?"

Vic didn't know which path to take. She could lie outright, and tell him that she didn't find him attractive, that he was nothing more than a client to her, that she was well aware that it could never work out between them in any long term way. Or she could tell him the truth, that the mere thought of him kept her awake some nights.

"Are you attracted to me, Vic?"

"Yes," she replied softly. Then, with wary a smile, she added, "God help me. I am."

Drew sighed, then slowly moved toward her, his lips hovering just over hers.

"Drew." His name escaped her lips on the warm wings of her breath, just before he kissed her.

"Stay with me?" he asked with a raspy whisper, their lips still touching slightly.

"What?" She couldn't think.

"In Florida. Say you'll stay in Florida."

She moved in for one more taste of him before his meaning settled on her and made its way to her logical mind.

"Stay in Florida?" she repeated. "I can't stay in Florida."

"You can," Drew stated. "We'll run the business together. See where this thing between us goes, how it plays out."

It caused her physical pain to pull away from him, as if he were a bandage fastened firmly to her skin.

"I can't stay here indefinitely, Drew. I have a life back at home. I have a job that I've worked my entire career to attain. You can't expect me to walk away from that."

Drew looked suddenly like a boy to her, with that sleepy, smoky look in his eyes, and his hair mussed and fallen down across his brow.

"It was always understood, Drew. You know that I'm only here to—"

"Save my business," he interrupted. "I know. A business I couldn't care less about if I worked at it."

An electrical pain shocked in her temple, and Vic reached up involuntarily to rub the spot. "Wh-what do you mean by that?"

"I mean, I haven't been entirely honest with you, Victoria."

When he called her by her full name, it sent a rush of heat through her entire body.

"My heart isn't in the business," he said after a long, floating silence. "I'll admit that."

"Then what harm would it do to sell it and come to New York?"

"I don't belong in New York, Victoria. Surely you know that about me now."

But I don't belong in Florida either.

"My father was a romantic," he continued. "The business was the brainchild of my mother. Trenton financed it, but my father, he built it for her. Just the way he built that house you saw the other day."

"Then why can't—"

"Because it was his legacy to me. It was what he wanted for me. And I've got everything tied up in seeing it succeed."

"I know about the mortgage you took out on the house," she

revealed, and Drew looked instantly stunned. "I'm sorry if that makes you feel invaded, but it was an accident that I found out, Drew. So we build the business into something really great, we get it thriving and vital, and then you sell it. And come to New York with me."

"And what about the house?" he asked her bitterly. "I sell that too?"

"Well . . ."

"No, Vic," he retorted. "My parents are buried there. It's the only home I've ever known."

"And New York is the only home I've ever known."

"Is it really the city you're so attached to?" he asked her. "Or is it that ridiculous job you're obsessed about?"

"Ridiculous?"

Streaks of anger flashed through her in electrical jolts, and Vic turned her entire body toward Drew.

"I'm sorry. I shouldn't have said that—"

"I've been working toward that *ridiculous job* for the whole of my adult life, Andrew Nolan! Do you have any idea what it's like to strive for something in everything you do, every day of your life? No, of course you don't! You've never had a spark of ambition or an ember of drive ignite inside you once, ever!"

"Vic—"

"You don't actually want the business to succeed," she accused him, hot flames of rage burning her words up to the surface. "Because that would mean you'd have to work for a living and not traipse around the beach with your friends, drinking smoothies all day and tossing a ball for your psychotic dog!"

"You don't know the first thing about what kind of man I am, sweetheart," he refuted angrily. "Or what I may or may not—"

"No!" she spouted. "No! You're right. I don't know you, Drew. And yet you would ask me to give up everything I've ever worked for and move to Florida and—"

"You're right!" he seethed. "I was out of my mind! Any man who could ever think for five seconds about building a life with the likes of you would have to be out of his mind."

And there they were, the magic words.

The sharp edge of those words cut so deep into her that Vic

couldn't even find breath, much less words to fling back at him. Flashes of Richard's rejection igniting before her eyes, she cranked back the door handle and flung the door open.

"Where do you think you're going?"

Away from you! she thought, but the words still couldn't escape from beneath the battle wounds bleeding inside her.

"Victoria, get back in this car!"

Flinging one foot firmly in front of the other, she stalked away from the car into the darkness where the stream of tears cascading defiantly down her face would be concealed.

"Vic!"

She could barely hear him calling to her above the uncontrollable sobs propelling themselves up from the deepest parts of her, but she refused to let him see that he'd wounded her; refused to allow him the satisfaction.

With her next step, Vic teetered, then tumbled; she was falling, falling, falling, until she landed with a splash in the murky slime of a roadside swamp.

Chapter Fourteen

"Give me your hand!"

"No!" she screamed for the second time, punctuating it with a violent splash of water toward him.

"I'm trying to help you," he offered softly, but Vic wasn't about to allow it. "Give me your hand."

"I told you, no! Just get away from me!"

"Alright," he said through clenched teeth. "Just stay there and drown, you infantile brat! Or be eaten by an alligator. I don't care."

Alligators?

Fear shot through her like a bullet, and Vic looked around into the darkness in every direction. Alligators weren't something she had considered.

When it sounded as if he might be preparing to walk away, she let out a little scream of frustration before surrendering. "Are you going to help me out of here?!"

"Are you going to give me your hand?"

Vic tossed her hand upward like an unwanted rag. "Well, take it."

She heard Drew release a ragged sigh before he found her. Taking her by the wrist, he yanked her upward, and she felt her feet leave her shoes in the stubborn mud beneath her.

"My shoes!" she cried as he pulled her from the water.

"Leave them."

Her bare feet had no sooner touched the gravel when Drew swooped her up into his arms and grudgingly began carrying her back toward the car.

"Put me down!" she demanded. "I can walk."

Without a word, he dropped her to her feet like a sack of potatoes, then stalked away. After just a moment, she heard the car door slam, and then she was instantly blinded by the white stream of the headlights.

The gravel beneath her feet made it difficult to make her way back, but she hobbled along on legs of rubber in fervent hope that she wouldn't slip down the embankment again. When she finally made it back to the car, her door was barely shut before Drew threw the car into motion and sped down the road.

The stench of mildew and mud permeated her nostrils, and Vic could hardly stand herself on the silent drive back. When they reached the parking lot and Drew turned off the motor, she immediately climbed out of the car and limped up the stairs. She hadn't even reached the top when he started the motor one more time and sped away into the night.

Vic didn't even take the time to peel off her clothes before she stepped beneath the warm spray of the shower. She had to relieve herself of the coat of slime covering her as soon as possible.

As the water cascaded over her, she cringed as clumps of unidentifiable gook fell at her feet. Snatching up the bar of soap in the porcelain tray built into the wall, she began to frantically scrub her hands, her face, her clothes—until she finally reached the stage where she could begin shedding her clothing.

One by one, the garments clunked to the floor of the tub, and she stood there under the water, scouring her skin with soap. After she'd shampooed her hair for the third time, she scrubbed herself again, just for good measure.

More than half an hour later, Vic slicked her clean hair back from her face and slipped into a short cotton nightgown and a thick pair of socks. With the cup of tea she'd just brewed, and the lit cigarette she couldn't seem to do without, she curled into the chair by the window and stared silently out toward the Gulf. She couldn't actually see it, as dark as it was, but she knew it was there. And for some strange reason that comforted her.

Raising the cigarette toward her lips, Vic noticed her own hand trembling, and it made her angry. In fact, as the recall button on her memory brought the entire evening undulating before her, her stomach knotted up and her heart throbbed at such a pace that she began to envision the impending cardiac arrest she didn't have the energy to battle against.

And then came the quick snippets of Drew. His hand outstretched to her from the murky shore; his smoky eyes, brimming with desire for her, as he confessed his feelings; then the harsh words that had sliced her open from head to toe. She knew Drew had no way of knowing how those words had transported her instantly back to the feelings of rejection and loss associated with Richard, but she was furious with him just the same.

Any man who could ever think for five seconds about building a life with the likes of you would have to be out of his mind.

Humiliation pressed in on her until she could hardly stand it any more, and yet the words played again and again in her head. Just as the urge to run away from them had overpowered her out beside that swamp, the same inclination nibbled at her now.

Vic stamped the cigarette out into the ashtray on the table beside her, and then steadied her shaking hands to immediately light another. She could call the airline that very night and be on a plane home the next morning. It would take her all of an hour to pack her things and . . .

Her train of thought derailed instantly as Tiffany jumped onto the tracks. Vic realized that she may not be much in the game of relationships, but she was the MVP when it came to business. She'd never left a project unfinished in her entire career, and Tiffany was counting on her to see this thing through.

Not to mention Drew.

She didn't want to think of him again, but there was no avoiding it. Aside from anything else that had occurred between them, he was the client, and she was here to do a job.

Once again she realized she didn't want to care, but she did. He'd wagered everything he had on this one shot to save Romantic Overtures; granted, it was a business he couldn't have cared less about, as it turned out, but he had so very much to lose if her efforts failed.

Vic twisted the cigarette in the ashtray and pressed out the burning ember. With a ragged sigh, she clenched her eyes shut and laid her head back to rest against the chair. She was dizzy from the nicotine, and just the slightest bit nauseated. Not wanting to think any more, about Drew or business or even cigarettes, she forced herself up and out of the chair and padded off to bed.

Her desperate need for sleep was overshadowed by the

voices of her past, and Vic tossed and turned for hours. Daybreak found her lying quietly on her back, tracing the patterns of the textured ceiling into mindless designs. When she realized that one of them bore a striking, if somewhat mystifying, resemblance to the shape of Drew's mouth, she instantly catapulted herself out of bed and into the bathroom.

Her clothes were still heaped on the floor of the tub, and she found herself repulsed by the very sight of them. After retrieving a plastic trash bag from the kitchen shelf, and a pair of rubber gloves from beneath the sink, she scooped up the outfit she had once treasured and dropped it into the bag. Dragging the wet load through the apartment, she mourned the $400 Fendi shoes that had once meant so much to her and were still lodged in the mud where she was forced to leave them. At the front door, Vic shed the thick yellow gloves and tossed them into the bag as well, knotting it off and dropping it to the floor.

Ten minutes later, donning her most comfortable pair of sweats, she snatched up her cigarettes and the trash bag, and headed out the door. She didn't look back, or even slow down, as she heaved the bag over the side of the trash bin.

Sunup was a beautiful sight over the water, and Vic climbed atop the nearest picnic table and sat cross-legged to watch it. Welcoming this new day seemed like a chore to her somehow, and the cigarette she raised to her lips seemed to weigh a hundred pounds.

"I thought you'd given that up," Pen said as she approached her, and Vic forced a heavy smile to the corners of her mouth when she reached the table area.

"Several times," she replied, flicking the lighter and taking in a long drag of smoke.

"You're up and at it awfully early this morning," the woman observed, planting herself at the corner of the bench below her. "Everything alright?"

"Couldn't sleep."

Vic didn't feel like talking, and part of her wished that Penelope would sense that and just be on her way. But it was just one more hope dashed, and Vic blew out a long trail of smoke on the wings of a weary sigh as Pen settled back against the table and stared out at the water, as if she were planning to stay awhile.

"Here. Have some."

The sound of Penelope's voice was like velvet sweeping across her, and Vic turned toward her to find a steaming Thermos cup being extended in her direction. The scent of fresh coffee caused her to salivate, and she silently took it from Penelope's hand.

"You know," the woman said softly as she poured a second cup for herself, "if you need a friend, I'm a pretty good candidate."

Vic took one last drag from her cigarette, then edged out the fire against a metal stud in the tabletop. The warm liquid felt lovely as it slipped down the back of her throat, and Vic closed her eyes for a moment.

"He's not the easiest man in the world to love, but Drew is a good man. With a good heart."

Vic's eyes jolted open and darted toward Penelope. "Who said I love him at all?"

"No one. It's just a hunch."

Vic let that sink in as her gaze drifted off toward the sunrise. Falling in love with Andrew Nolan was the last thing on earth she would ever have allowed herself to do. What an absurd leap for Penelope to have made!

"You've spoken to him then."

"Yes," she replied.

A flush of heat fanned out from the center of her stomach, tickling its way up to the very top of Vic's head.

"Is that why you're here? To mediate between the two of us?"

"No," Penelope said with a chuckle. "I'm here to see the sunrise. Finding you here too was just a lucky surprise."

Lucky.

"I thought you were more into sunsets than sunrises," Vic said without looking back at her.

"The wonder of God's hand on the universe, either waking it up or putting it to sleep, is a magnificent thing, Victoria. They both accomplish the same thing. It's much the same as love."

Vic swept the woman a momentary sideways glance.

"It's who you love that's important. Not the geography of where you love them."

Very subtle, Vic thought bitterly.

"What are you trying to say to me, Penelope?" she finally asked. "You think I should give up the life I've worked to make in New York, just because someone asks me to?"

"No," the other woman replied thoughtfully. "That's not what I'm saying at all."

What then? What are you trying to say?

"My concern is that nothing is missed. For either you or Andrew. Sometimes we look so hard to see the forest that we miss the beauty of the individual trees. Look out there," she said, pointing toward the horizon. "Tell me what you see."

Vic looked, and then shrugged. "I see a beautiful sunrise."

"Yes, it is beautiful," she concurred. "But do you know what I see?"

"What?"

"I see the blush of pink across the cheekbones of an infant sky. I see the reflection of a crescent moon fading away into the orange sun of a new day. I see a new beginning, Victoria." And with that, she gently squeezed Vic's hand and graced her with a smile that brought tears up into her eyes. "It's all in how you look at things."

Penelope's eyes were warm and brown and comforting, like hot chocolate on a cold New York morning. And despite the pinch of rebellion Vic felt at the message that had been delivered, she couldn't ignore the wisdom within it. It had been such a long time since she'd had a talk with her mother, and yet the reminder of the consolation she'd always been able to find in her wasn't lost on Vic. There was a special maternal-type something that just seemed to ooze out of Penelope, and it was almost irresistible.

"Do you know how Drew and I met?" she asked, drawing Vic's focus back to the moment.

"I don't think so. No."

"He was taking a class I was teaching. It was a study on how passages of literature have historically molded and shaped public views. In the first couple of classes, we had examined

Shakespeare and Twain and Hemingway. And then one afternoon, I brought out a Bible and began reading a passage out of
the book of Isaiah."

One corner of Vic's mouth curled into an awkward smile. "I
never really thought of the Bible as, you know, literature."

"This was Andrew's view as well," she said with a laugh.
"Oh, and the boy was ready to fight it to the death!"

"Really?" Vic tried to imagine Drew in the classroom that
day, and she wondered what his motivation had been. Didn't he
believe in God?

" 'Don't you believe in God?' I asked him," Penelope continued, as if reading her mind. " 'That's not the point!' he
countered!"

Vic giggled out loud at that. Penelope had Drew's manner-
isms down pat!

"And I told him he was right, that wasn't the point. No matter what his belief system, The Bible had been in print longer
than any other single example of the written word. People were
moved by it, they memorized passages from it, and some even
adjusted their lifestyles to conform to the messages it con-
veyed. Now, if that's not a powerful piece of literature, tell me
what is!"

"And what did he say?"

"Well, we all debated the issue throughout the class. And
then Drew and I continued the discussion over coffee, and he
and I have been exchanging ideas ever since."

Vic shook her head and released a rolling chuckle that did
her heart some good. Funny how the thought of Drew taking
classes at the university seemed so foreign to her. She hadn't
thought him the type.

"That same passage from the book of Isaiah that brought
Drew and I together in the first place comes to mind this morning, Victoria."

She looked at Penelope warily, the grin melting from her
face and an unexplained seriousness creeping up from her
heart.

" 'For my thoughts are not your thoughts, neither are your
ways my ways.' This passage of scripture simply states that

there is a bigger picture sometimes. That we can have a preconceived notion in our minds because of our past, our childhood, because of broken friendships or love affairs, but sometimes there is a higher thought, a different purpose for our lives than we were able to imagine. Being open to those possibilities is part of embracing the wonder of life."

Vic let her gaze slide away from Penelope and bounce along the shore until it finally came to rest on a clump of feathery white clouds dotting the blue horizon. The watercolors of the morning had slipped away and a crisp cerulean sky had taken their place. It was indeed a new day.

For a moment, Vic almost wanted to believe that there were possibilities along with it, chances for the rift between she and Drew to be magically bridged. There were, after all, deep feelings brewing between the two of them, and perhaps, for her, a fresh opportunity for love and commitment and a future with a man unlike any other she'd ever known.

And then the doubts rose from the mist once again. The impossible obstacles. The harsh words. The facts.

Crestfallen, Vic rose to her feet and handed Penelope the empty plastic cup.

"Thanks for the coffee," she said sadly. "And for the history lesson."

"Any time."

Vic trudged across the sand toward the office. She wondered if Drew was even up yet as she took the stairs to her apartment, noting the distinct absence of Louie at her heels.

Slumping into the chair she'd taken to occupying whenever some serious thinking needed to be done, Vic instinctively reached into her pocket for a cigarette. She pulled one out of the pack and stared at it for a moment, then tossed it, along with the half-empty package, onto the table beside her.

She groaned as Penelope's words rattled around inside her head, then fell silent except for a few shallow breaths as her mind drifted over the events of the prior evening. In only an instant, she was back there again, in the driver's seat of his car, his hands stoking the fire deep in her body, his lips coaxing embers into roaring flames.

The physical attraction between them couldn't be denied, Vic knew that. From the moment she'd seen him sitting in the conference room back in New York, even if she hadn't recognized it then, she'd been enthralled. Everything about Andrew Nolan appealed to her, from his long and lanky frame to the deep set of his ivy-colored eyes and the inviting curve of amusement seemingly emblazoned upon his lips. His was a smile that always seemed to reveal traces of secrets he had no business knowing.

He could be infuriating, that was true. But he could also be insightful and sweet, and kinder than any man she'd ever met. Her thoughts took the form of a movie trailer recounting their relationship—the look on his face the day she'd discovered him mocking her down in the office; their dance at Tiffany's engagement party; the kiss that followed that very night in the car; Vic's hands around his waist as he led her through the dark apartment the night of the storm; the sadness in his eyes at the sight of the tombstones standing beneath the banyan tree in the back yard of his family home. And beneath it all, a hauntingly familiar soundtrack, music that set her pulse to pounding. It was a symphony of sorts, where electricity took the place of the woodwinds; affection, the form of the strings. It was the music of her heart, and Vic could no more deny the love there than she could deny her own desire to refute it.

I . . . love . . . him.

She was in love with Drew Nolan.

The thought pierced straight through her with a sort of stunned tremor that cleared her head and fogged it—all in the same moment.

But how could she love him?

All of the obstacles danced before her eyes: New York versus Florida, corporate versus non-corporate, drive versus . . . a lack thereof. He was a bit of a slacker, she had to admit, and she was anything but. A life with Drew would mean more than just compromise. It could mean settling. And it could mean loss.

But it would also mean . . . *love.*

Wasn't it possible, she asked herself, that they could work together to solve the seemingly insurmountable obstacles standing between them? If Drew was feeling for her even half of what she was feeling for him . . .

All of the stumbling blocks in the road between her door and Drew's dissolved as Vic rose from her chair and walked out the front door. Three gentle knocks on his door, and she braced herself for what was to come. Vic wasn't prone to impulsive behavior, she never had been, but when Drew's door opened, and he stood there facing her curiously, his rumpled hair fallen across his brow and that luscious mouth curved upward on one side questioningly, she did the only thing her body would allow her to do.

She stepped forward, wrapped her arms around his neck and kissed him for all she was worth.

"I say *po-tay-to*, you say *po-tah-to,* is that it?" Drew asked her curiously when she was through, enunciating for effect.

"What are you talking about?" she asked with a giggle, her arms still clasped tightly around his neck.

"My e-mail," he replied.

"What e-mail?"

Drew froze for a moment and looked into Vic's crackling eyes.

"Vic, listen," he said as he began to pull away. "I wrote you an e-mail this morning about how I was feeling, about—"

"No!" she shouted. "No more words. Words are our enemy!"

"No, listen, you don't understand—"

"Here's what I understand," she cried, pulling him toward her shamelessly. "I don't need to understand anything else right now, Drew. And neither do you."

"Vic—"

"Shhhhh," she meowed at him. "Shut up and kiss me."

Her lips pressed his softly at first, and then came the rush of heat one more time. "Is there anything else you feel the need to say right at this moment?"

After a moment of silence, he replied, "Not a thing."

Chapter Fifteen

"Come in here and talk to me," Vic said, leading Drew into his apartment by the hand.

"I thought words are our enemy," he replied with a grin.

"Oh, that. Yeah, well, what I meant was . . . *your* words are our enemy. Not mine."

"Oh, oh, I see," he said with a swell of laughter while following close behind her.

"And speaking of words, what was that you said about an e-mail?"

Drew's heart began to pound. "I sent it this morning," he admitted, steeling his arms in an effort to keep her right where she was.

"What did it say?"

The questioning in her eyes was almost more than he could stand.

"I gave you a whole list of reasons why we . . . you and I . . . could never work."

"You did?"

There was the struggle he'd anticipated! Drew held Vic to him as if she were captured in a vice.

"Drew, let me go," she said softly, and he did so reluctantly. "You don't think we can work?"

"Well, I didn't last night. But—"

"Now?"

"Now. I hope we can."

"Me too," she said so softly that he almost didn't hear her, and he tried not to register surprise when she squirmed back into his embrace and snuggled her face into the curve of his neck.

"Vic, listen—"

"Shhhhh," she told him softly. "No more words just now. Okay?"

Drew kissed the top of her head gently and closed his eyes. "Okay."

"Do you feel like pizza?" Drew asked, and Vic turned up her nose in reply.

"How about Chinese?"

"Fine by me."

"I have a take-out menu next door. I'll go over and grab it."

Vic watched Louie scamper down the stairs and around the corner before walking into her apartment. She stopped into the bathroom to splash some water on her face and run a brush through her hair, then snatched up the take-out menu from the kitchen table and headed for the door.

A sudden thought struck her, and she turned back and looked at her laptop on the dining room table as she stood in the gaping doorway. Despite the warning bells sounding inside her head, she cautiously crossed the room again and sat down at the computer.

"You've got mail."

"Don't I know it," she told the announcement, then clicked on the third of nearly a dozen.

From *drew.nolan@romanticovertures.com*
Dear Vic.

Something told her not to read it, and she tried to resist, but curiosity got the better of her, and she scrolled down into the body of the message.

I hope you've recovered from your dip in the swamp last night. Not one of Florida's finest attributes, I'm afraid, and I'm very sorry for what sent you over the edge into it. Things should never have escalated to those—

"Hey! What're you doing?"

Vic's head jerked toward the sound of Drew's voice so violently that her neck cracked in two different places.

"No, no, no, no, no," he insisted as he jogged toward her and captured her wrist and the computer mouse beneath his hand.

"I just wanted to see what you had to say," she reasoned. "Don't you think it's something we should talk about?"

"No, I do not!" he exclaimed. "Words are our enemy, remember?"

"Just your words," she reminded him with the hint of a smile.

"Right. And these are my words. I reserve the right to denounce them at will."

"Drew—"

"No. Victoria, don't read this."

Their eyes locked together for several beats before she sighed and allowed her hand to fall limp beneath his still-firm grasp.

"Go on. Click on the delete button."

"Delete?" she objected, her grip over the mouse turning severe once more.

"Delete," he repeated, and she noted a flash of desperation that deepened the hue of his emerald eyes. "Do it."

"This must be a doozy of an e-mail," she commented as she shook his hand free from hers and moved the mouse until it reached the delete button at the top of the screen. "You're sure?"

"Do it."

Poking her tongue out at him playfully, Vic pushed down on the left side of the mouse.

"Are you sure you want to delete this file?" she read to him from the prompt on the monitor.

"Yes," he stated immediately.

"Yes," she repeated, clicking it away.

Drew wrapped his arms around her from behind and planted a kiss firmly on the top of her head before reaching out and folding down the laptop screen until it snapped shut.

"Now," he said seriously, guiding her out of the chair and into his arms, "I need nourishment."

"Bourbon chicken?"

"And lots of it."

Vic's stomach rumbled as she dialed the number at the top of the menu, initiating an ordering frenzy that resulted in a virtual Oriental feast. The delivery came in two large bags and consisted of bourbon chicken, pork lo mein, tiny barbecued spare ribs, assorted types of fried rice, several egg rolls and half a dozen fortune cookies.

Drew paid the driver while Vic searched for her shoes; Louie joined them out of nowhere on the trek across the sand toward the picnic tables at the edge of the beach. They unloaded the substantial banquet onto the tabletop just in time to take the first bites to the backdrop of a spectacular sunset.

Vic recalled the start to the day with a grin. All had seemed so lost, so hopeless, when she'd shared that lone cup of coffee with Penelope. All the talk of bigger pictures and higher thoughts! She paused for a moment to wonder whether there really was a God high above her, beyond that emblazoned sky, moving things around like little chess pieces just to make this unexpected path to love a little straighter, a little smoother.

What a difference a day makes, she marveled.

She plucked up a chunk of chicken between two chopsticks and offered it happily to Drew. He took it, and then lifted his egg roll to her lips in return.

"Mmm, needs plum sauce," she informed him through a full mouth.

"I think I saw some here."

She watched him clamor through the cookies and napkins until he produced a small plastic container from inside the bag. Dipping his egg roll into it, he offered her a second taste.

"Oooh, that's more like it," she swooned. "Wow, this is good!"

"You're just starving."

"I am. But it's still magnificent."

Drew plopped the last of his egg roll into his mouth and chewed it quickly. He'd barely taken time to swallow it before he moved in toward her, pulling her face to his with both hands.

"You're beautiful," he said on a whisper, and then touched her lips with a lingering kiss.

"And you're delicious," she said when they were through.

"It's the plum sauce," he grinned. "It makes all the difference."

When they had each eaten more than their fill, there was still enough food left over to nourish a small band of hungry thieves. Vic began closing up containers and re-packing the plastic bags.

"What are you doing?" Drew asked her softly.

"Leftovers," she replied. "There's nothing like Chinese food for breakfast."

When he didn't answer, she looked over her shoulder at him to find a partly amused, partly disgusted expression on his beaming face.

"Your stepfather wasn't kidding, was he? You treat your body like an adversary."

"Yeah, yeah, yeah."

"Let's head home," he suggested after a few minutes more.

"Okay," she purred, but didn't make a move. "Whatever you say."

"Yeah," he said with a chuckle. "That'll be the day."

Vic pulled back from him and grimaced. "Are you saying I'm stubborn, Nolan?"

"I believe that's what I'm saying, Townsend, yes," he replied. "Stubborn and willful . . . and rebellious."

"You think name-calling is going to get you anywhere with me?" she asked him, struggling to press down the laughter threatening to burst free at any moment.

"And focused and driven and intelligent . . ."

"Well," she sputtered, rising to her feet and backing away from him slightly. "That's more like it."

"And adorable, and wild, and . . ." he continued, rising slowly, and taking a few steps toward her.

"And?" she cried just before springing into a full run toward the water.

"And fast!" he exclaimed, setting out after her.

Vic was knee-deep in the surf, and nearly breathless, when Drew finally reached her. She nearly swooned with exhilaration when he grabbed her by the forearm and reeled her around to face him. Defending herself, she used her free hand to frantically splash him.

"And gorgeous and sensual and irresistible," he continued in a low growl, pulling her into a kiss that spiraled its way downward into every corner of her body.

Although neither of them had spoken the words outright, choruses of "I love you" had been ringing like persistent church bells in the distance throughout her time with Drew. However, as much as she hated the idea of it, Vic had been beckoned out

of her love-soaked haze and back to the business at hand. Devon's crew would be arriving that very afternoon, and there was
still a lot of planning to do.

"They'll want to shoot you and Walter together," she told
Tiffany over the telephone that morning. "Don't be afraid to
wear something a little daring, but remember it's a family show.
We'll want to really play up the contrast between the two of
you. Oh, and Tiff? We probably don't want to mention that you
work for Drew occasionally. It gives it too much of a homespun
feeling to the whole thing. You're just another one of his many
clients in the greater St. Petersburg area."

"Got it!" Tiffany sounded as if she'd accompanied the ac-
knowledgement with a salute. "Anything else, Boss?"

"Just be your lovely and adorable self. Except don't be late. I
need you here at the office by two."

"Affirmative. Fourteen hundred hours."

"All right, you. I get the dig. I'm not trying to be bossy. I just
want this to go right."

"Sir, yes, sir! As do I, sir."

"Hanging up on you now."

"Letting you."

Vic was grinning from ear to ear when she disconnected the
call. Wasting no time, she scurried out of the conference room
and into the front office. The cleaning team was just finishing
up and she beamed at the results.

No sooner had the front door opened, punctuating the departure of the last of the janitorial crew, than a rush of high-pitched
barks and growls moved into full swing.

"Louie! Can it!"

"You've got to do something about him," she yelled over
Louie's outraged monologue.

"What would you suggest?" Drew asked, yanking at the
dog's collar and sliding him across the floor away from the
door.

"A tranquilizer comes to mind," she quipped. "But at the
very least, could you lock him in your apartment? We can't
have him running around like this while they're taping."

"Your wish is my command. I'll take him across the street for a quick run, and then I'll send him off to solitary confinement."

"Thank you."

Anointing her with a quick cascade of kisses, Drew released Louie and the two of them disappeared out the front door.

Vic checked her watch: 10:30. She still had a couple of hours before the crew arrived. Grabbing a bottle of iced tea from the fridge on her way, she settled down at the conference room table and lifted the lid of her laptop.

Double-clicking on the mail file on the desktop, she scrolled through the list in search of something from Sasha. She'd promised the final artwork on Tiffany's dress before noon.

Several messages from Krissy were accompanied by a few office memos and a note from Trenton. Looking its little head out from above all of the business-related e-mails of the last week that she hadn't made time to sort through, Vic noticed the one line that stood out from the rest.

From: drew.nolan@romanticovertures.com.
Subject: About last night.

It didn't dawn on her that this could be the same email Drew had forced her to delete from her inbox without ever reading it, or that it could have been downloaded to the file on her desktop anyway. Carelessly, she clicked it open, and the email appeared on the screen before her.

Dear Vic,
I hope you've recovered from your dip in the swamp last night. Not one of Florida's finest attributes, I'm afraid, and I'm very sorry for what sent you over the edge into it. Things should never have escalated to those levels, and I take full responsibility for what happened to you.

A sudden rush of adrenaline soared through her, and icy fingers of dread meandered up her spine. This *was* the email she'd deleted.

I would also like to apologize for the ridiculous and hurtful things I said to you. They were words said in anger, and not something I actually meant. A man would be lucky to have the love of someone like you, Vic, and I hope that when you find the right guy he can appreciate the many things in you that make you so unique. You deserve someone like that.

Vic grinned as she paused to take a drink from the bottle of tea she still clutched in one hand. She did deserve someone like that. And now she'd found him! It seemed silly that Drew hadn't wanted her to read this. It was quite sweet, actually.

As for any talk of an actual future with me, I only hope you can excuse it away like an unexpected belch after a meal.

Something dropped into the pit of her stomach, and the clunk of it startled her. He compared the idea of their coupling to . . . a burp? She read it again. . . . *like an unexpected belch after a meal.*

You were so right in your reaction to such a preposterous idea. The thought of us getting together is absurd. It could never happen.

Absurd? Preposterous? A familiar queasiness knotted up inside her, and she thought for a moment about hitting the delete button and not reading the rest. Discarding the notion, she swallowed hard and read on.

You are a beautiful woman, Victoria, and the man in me has responded to that. Although I would like to think I'm a little deeper than my baser desires, I have to admit to you that I'm not always. Everything you said about the differences between us was right on the money! Despite the gratification we might have had for a while, you and I both know it would have ended with you getting on a plane and going back to your real life where you belong. And I would stay here, where I belong.

"Oh. Drew."
Her worst fears reared their ugly head. She'd shoved them down as far as she could manage over the last few days, but here they were again. Alive and verbose, spouting their secrets as boldly as they knew how.

You were wise to laugh in the face of the suggestion that we could ever overcome the huge differences between us, and I think it would be a disservice to both of us to confuse reality with fun and games.

Fun and games. The words sliced cleanly through her heart, like a glistening steel knife down the center of an apple. Oh, why hadn't she stopped reading while she was ahead? Drew had trusted her not to read words that he'd written in haste when hope for the two of them was just a distant song. Things had changed since he'd written these words. Her heart told her not to betray his trust, to delete the email without reading another word. But still, she was drawn to continue.

I'm not about to become a New Yorker, and trying to make you fit into my world would be a little like transplanting the Empire State Building to the lot across from The Beachside. In the light of day, the whole idea is rather laughable, actually.
I don't know if it's possible, but could we please try and forget this nonsense . . .

"Nonsense?" It stung like a bee on a clover. No wonder he hadn't wanted her to read it.

. . . and get back to what really matters? I need you to be focused on the task you came down here to accomplish: saving my sorry excuse for a business before you go back and take that job you've been working toward for so long. You belong in that corner office with the window over Central Park. And I belong here, with my family home safe once more. That is reality. Anything else, although potentially enjoyable for a moment . . .

That's what we are doing here? she thought. *Enjoying a moment?*

. . . can't carry over into the real world. You were so right.
Drew.

Vic read the last paragraph over several times.

She didn't know how long she sat there in stunned silence after that. The words swirled on the screen before her against the diametrically opposed gears of her own churning thoughts.

Oh, what had she done? She'd given her heart to someone who saw their possible pairing as nothing more than a diversion. A surrender to carnal impulses that were shatteringly powerful, but still "laughable" and "absurd" in the reflection of a future.

"Where are you hiding, woman?" Drew called out as he came through the front door. "We've got things to do!"

Vic clicked quickly to close the email and watched it disappear from the screen. Guilt simmered at the pit of her stomach as it vanished, and she considered the idea of confessing her accidental discovery so that they could laugh away what he had written; so that she could breathe again.

"What are you doing?" he asked from the doorway.

"Ch-checking for Sasha's artwork," she lied, steeling herself against the black cloud of emotion that hung overhead, threatening to break loose with one of those unanticipated Florida storms. "It's not here yet. I'll have to call her."

"Well, get on it then. I'll call and check the details for the rehearsal dinner."

"Okay."

Vic didn't move a muscle. She just stared into the air before her in hopes that some of it would make its way into her lungs and up to her brain.

"Vic? Sweetheart?"

She blinked hard and then shot a glance toward the door.

"Yes?"

"Are you all right?"

"Y-yes. Fine."

Snatching up the phone, she began to quickly dial.

"Sasha, it's Victoria Townsend. I haven't received your art, and I've got the *Knot* crew here in an hour."

Chapter Sixteen

In less than two weeks' time, everything had changed for Romantic Overtures. Vic had updated the website to a slick promotional fare stocked with pictures and quotes and prosaic scenarios, all bulging with the promise of originality and romance, and the site had taken more than a thousand hits in the course of just a few days. Tiffany was becoming a bit of a celebrity in her own right, being touted as "The New Face of Millennial Romance" in the promos *Tying the Knot* seemed to be running every hour, and her wedding hadn't even taken place yet.

"Just go to RomanticOvertures-dot-com," Vic's voice spouted from the answering machine in the reception office. "Your dreams await!"

"The phone is ringing right off the hook!" Tiffany exclaimed. "Can you imagine what it will do once the show actually airs next week?"

"Well, that was the point of all this," Vic assured her.

"Drew must be over the moon. Where is he, anyway?"

"He's meeting with someone out at the Don Cesar."

"That big, beautiful hotel on the beach?" Tiffany cried. "That place is amazing."

"Apparently very big into weddings, too. They want to work out a promotional deal."

"Things have really taken off for this place, Vic. You've done what you said you could do, in spades."

"It's my business," she stated without emotion. "It's what I do."

"Oooh, I had my final fitting for the dress yesterday. I wish you could have been there to see it! It's perfect, Vic. Sasha is a dream."

"I'm glad," Vic said with a sigh, leaning back in her chair and taking her first breather since dawn. "Are you all ready to become someone's wife this evening?"

"More than ready. I can hardly stand the wait."

"The camera crew is going to be with you out there at four,"

Vic told her. "I can't get free until around five, but I'll be there in plenty of time. And you'll have Penelope if you need anything."

"Are you driving out to the beach with Drew?"

"I don't know," she replied thoughtfully. "We haven't had time to talk about it."

"He sure is happy these days," Tiffany observed, and Vic took note of the curious arch to her pierced eyebrow. "Would you have anything to do with that?"

Vic lifted one shoulder in a non-committal shrug before rising to her feet and opening her arms to Tiffany.

"Come here," she said. "I want to give you a hug."

"What's this for?" Tiffany asked her from within the embrace.

"You are a doll, and I want you to know how much I appreciate you."

"Are you kidding?" Tiffany stepped back and looked at Vic seriously. "You're the one who has made all of this happen. My wedding is going to be everything I ever dreamed it could be, and it's all because of you."

They hugged warmly one more time, and Vic planted a soft kiss on Tiffany's cheek.

"If I don't get the chance to tell you before you take your vows," she said, "be happy. You and Walter are a perfect fit."

"Opposites attract," the girl returned hopefully. "Let that be a lesson to you."

She had had too many lessons already, Vic thought. There wasn't room in her overwhelmed heart for even one more.

A while later, she ran a bath for herself upstairs and released a sigh from deep within her soul as she lowered herself into the fragrant bubbles. She'd been a mass of raw nerve endings for days on end, and the warmth of the water soothed her frayed edges.

She and Drew had been so wrapped up in riding the wave of progress that they'd barely had any time for themselves in the week since she'd accidentally read that wretched e-mail. But on the occasions that they'd spent any time alone, Vic had held firm to her promise not to think about the future, and she'd never admitted that she knew his thoughts about it.

She loved him. There had been no denying that, even after she'd opened the e-mail and read it for the first time. And there had been many times since that afternoon that she'd wanted to open it again and go over the words Drew had written, but she had finally deleted the copy from her desktop file to ensure her resistance. And with the push of a button, Vic had made herself a vow to never make him regret his time with her.

"I love you," she wanted to shout at him in her weakest moments, but she'd held the words back. How, she didn't know. But she had, and she always would.

She was going to enjoy every possible moment with Drew, Vic had pledged. And when she got on that plane and went back to New York, she would take her burgeoning declarations right along with her. She would smile a sexy little smile, thank him for the diversion from reality, and leave with her dignity intact. But in the meantime, she would savor every sacred touch and every loving kiss, and she would take those memories home with her.

They would be what kept her warm on those cold and lonely New York winter nights to come.

Drew could hardly contain himself throughout the ceremony. It was a tropical wonderland of romance and joy, so much more elegant and touching than what he had initially imagined at the suggestion of a W-themed wedding! The camera crew from *Tying the Knot* had captured it all, from the moments leading up to the vows right on through to the current one. And Vic had been instrumental in guiding them, so gently that Drew guessed they hadn't even felt her fingerprint on the project. She was a natural at what she did, he had to admit, but her business sense wasn't what intrigued him the most that day.

She had turned Tiffany's wedding into a unique mixture of intimacy and fan-fare; the event held an air of romance at every curve, and he had gladly allowed himself to be swept away on the breeze of it all—until emotion nearly gave way to an actual mist of tears at the proclamation of "husband and wife." That was where he drew the line, after all, and he reeled it back in with all that was left of his inner restraint.

Restraint?

The word seemed comical to him. Hadn't he really lost all claims on restraint more than a week ago? And what was more, he hadn't cared one iota.

Glancing across the aisle at Vic, he nearly lost it again. With the simple wave of her manicured hand as it brushed away a stray lock of raven-black hair from her porcelain face, she had moved him to the core.

My God, but she is beautiful.

She reminded him of a character in a book he'd read once while hiding in his favorite spot in the branches of the banyan tree. Amidst a tale of Robin Hood-type thieves involved in sword-drawn adventures, a maiden had appeared from across the wooden bridge. Victoria Townsend now took the shape of that fair maiden, her hair swept upward in a wavy array of bends and curls, dotted with tiny green rhinestone flowers, the very shade he'd imagined the forest trees to be in that novel he'd read so long ago.

Her dress was the palest mint green, and a gather of ribbed pleats fell to a sheer full skirt. The little capped sleeves of the dress exposed the milky softness of her long neck above a round, scooped neckline, and his gaze grew warm as it ran down the length of her smooth bare arms.

He watched her as she moved, and a wave of desire washed over him. If she was the beautiful Victorian-era Juliet that she appeared to be, then he was most certainly the Romeo who hoped to capture her heart.

When the intensity of the ceremony had died down into sheer festivity as the reception kicked into full gear, Drew continued to watch her. She was a vision; one he was determined to keep in place. Remembering the prize he'd hidden inside the breast pocket of his jacket, Drew made his way through the congratulatory crowd until he reached Vic, and he placed his hand on the small of her back. When she turned and glanced back at him, he saw a flicker of sadness dart over her crystalline eyes.

"Come with me," he whispered to her, and just the feel of her small hand as it slipped into his larger one sent a jolt of electricity straight through him.

He led her across the length of the tent, past the rows of candlelight pedestals that bordered the celebration. The Gulf rose and dropped to the nearby shore in consistent but passive measure, and the early evening breeze was balmy and inviting. It was the perfect moment, the one he'd been waiting for all day.

"Let's go for a walk," he suggested, and as she paused to slip her small feet out of the delicate clear slippers dotted with tiny green crystals that matched the ones in her hair, he moved the square treasure in his jacket to the pocket of his trousers for easier access. Following suit, he kicked off his own shoes and rolled his socks into balls inside one of them.

Vic's hand felt small to him as she clutched his and they padded along the softened sand, leaving footsteps into the foamy surf. The cool water felt good on his toes.

"It was a beautiful wedding," she said, and the sound of her voice caressed him like a song.

"It was."

A few more yards of silence, and then Drew stopped, turning Vic to face him. Taking her into his arms, he kissed her gently.

"Vic, I want to talk to you," he began, and then she smiled and nodded her head.

"I wanted to talk to you too."

"Do you want to go first?" he asked.

"Would you mind?"

"Ladies first."

Vic swallowed hard and then smiled awkwardly.

"I've really enjoyed this time with you, Drew."

"I'm glad to hear that," he replied, running two fingers up the length of her arm and pausing to caress a stray wisp of hair at the side of her face.

"You are such an amazing man," she continued. "So giving and sweet. I don't think I've ever enjoyed spending time with a man more."

"You've been quite enjoyable yourself," he teased.

Vic smiled at him, and he thought he saw gratitude flash in those amazing eyes of hers.

I should be the one who's grateful, he thought.

Reaching into the pocket of his trousers, he wrapped his hand around the small velvet box.

Ask her. Now's the perfect time to ask her.

"But I don't want you to think that I've mistaken this time for anything more than it is."

What?

"It's been absolutely perfect. But I think it's time to say what neither of us has wanted to say."

"And just what is that?" he asked as a twister of acid shot through his stomach.

"It's time to say goodbye."

"Goodbye? What? What are you talking about?"

She had to be kidding. Drew dropped the square box to the depth of his pocket and let his hand fall to rest over top of it.

"It's not like this could ever amount to anything more than it is, Drew. We both know that."

Running both hands through his hair, he tugged at his gaze until it slipped away from her and landed on a rolling wave approaching in the distance.

"I spoke to Trenton this morning, and he said that we've got a swell of new accounts that need attention right now. And with the business off and running the way it is, you're well on your way to firmer ground here."

"You're leaving then." He couldn't even look at her when he said it.

"I'm needed more back in New York."

Impossible. "I see."

"I want to thank you, Drew. I've had such a great time."

"Well, I'm all about having a good time," he said bitterly. "You know that."

"I've stopped smoking," she added with a hopeful glint.

"Thank God."

"And I feel great. I just . . . think the time has come."

"Yeah. No, you're right. The corner office awaits."

"Right," she said with a smile. "Creative Director of Marchant Media."

"That was the plan all along," he muttered. "But I sort of thought you'd begun to like it here. Begun to fit in."

"Me? In Florida?" she chuckled. "It was always absurd. I'm a New York City girl, through and through."

"You can take the girl out of the city, I guess . . ."

"Right."

"Well . . ."

"Yes."

"I guess that's it then," he said, then cast a hopeful glance her way. "You'll be leaving?"

"Yes. I'm going home."

Drew dragged both hands through his hair one more time, looking off toward the party in full swing up the beach. Someone appeared outside the tent just then. When she waved her arms over her head, he realized that it was Penelope.

"They're cutting the cake," she hollered through cupped hands.

"Okay," he returned, motioning toward her.

"We don't want to miss that."

"No," he replied. Then, offering his arm to Vic, he forced a smile to his anguished face. "Shall we?"

She took it, and they headed back toward the reception. And with each step he took, Drew felt something inside him die just a little.

Vic had hated the idea of goodbyes. So she'd stayed up late writing letters to Tiffany and Penelope, promising to keep in touch and thanking them for their friendship. Then, of course, there was the letter to Drew.

She'd agonized over it half the night and imagined that the delete key on the keyboard of her laptop hadn't gotten so much use in all the time she'd owned it. When she finally completed the e-mail and pushed the button to send it, she only had three hours left to pack her things and get out to Tampa International and turn in her rental car. She arrived at the airport just in time to check in an hour prior to the departure of the 8:00 A.M. flight to JFK.

Once in the air, the first thirty minutes of the flight were turbulent due to the sudden appearance of an unexpected Florida storm. No matter how she tried, she hadn't been able to see the ground through the thick carpet of blackened clouds beneath the plane. She'd known better than to try and look back anyway, but she couldn't seem to resist the effort. She'd spent the rest of the flight with her eyes closed, knowing full well that sleep wasn't going to come. How could it have inched its way in past Drew, the way he filled up her mind's eye like he did?

Upon arrival in New York, she took a taxi into the city. The doorman of her apartment building greeted her enthusiastically, welcoming her home several times over in the elevator up to her apartment, and then again after he'd dropped her bags and boxes just inside the door. She hadn't given Krissy any notice that she'd be returning, so it was no surprise that a thin coat of dust layered all of her furniture, and that her refrigerator was barren.

Standing at her living room window, staring out over the other brownstones that lined her street, Vic released the first stream of tears that had come since she'd rattled off her careless goodbye to Drew on the beach. And that first cascade of tears was unceasing, flowing constantly for the next several hours as she lay across her bed, clutching her pillow and wishing it were Drew.

"You look amazing!" Krissy crooned when she looked up from her desk and greeted Vic as she walked through the door.

"Thanks. It's good to see you again."

"No, I mean it! I wouldn't have known you on the street. You really look great, Vic."

"Thank you, Krissy." She tried not to let her irritation show. It wasn't Krissy's fault that she was back, after all.

"Wait until you see your new office! You're going to wet your pants!"

"I'll try to contain myself," she grinned, heading through the secretarial area toward the large mahogany door.

Victoria Townsend. Creative Director.

It was etched right into the glass of the door, just as she'd always imagined it.

The phone rang as she pumped the brass-handled door to her office and walked through.

"Victoria Townsend's office. How may I help you?" Krissy's voice echoed behind her.

Two of the four walls of the office were made of glass, from floor to ceiling. The other two were paneled half way up with a deep, rich mahogany that matched the enormous entry while a serene steel blue color stained the rest of the wall above the ornate chair rail molding. Her familiar desk and credenza were faced by a lush floral sofa and two midnight blue velvet wing-back chairs; a low claw-footed table displayed a crystal vase brimming with full-blooming roses between them. Beyond the windows, the city of New York welcomed her home in all its urban splendor, but Vic hardly flashed it a proper greeting.

She unloaded her briefcase and laptop to the credenza, then sank down into the leather chair.

"Mr. Marchant would like you to stop by his office once you're settled in," Krissy announced over the intercom. "And you've got a briefing with the creative staff scheduled for ten-thirty in the main conference room."

"Thank you, Krissy."

"Welcome back, Vic. It's really good to have you home."

She wanted to tell her it was good to be home, but she didn't have it in her to lie about one more thing.

"My girl, you look splendid!" Trenton declared when he looked up from behind his massive desk and saw her standing in the doorway. "Come in and sit down."

She folded into the nearest of the chairs on the other side of his desk and flashed him a smile.

"How have you been?" she asked.

"Never mind me. What about you? How did you find your office?"

"It's fine. Beautiful. Thank you, Trenton."

"And how are you feeling? Have you seen the company physician yet?"

"This afternoon at two," she placated him. "But all those

numbers will be right where you want them, I'm sure. I've quit smoking, and I've been eating reasonably well."

"Excellent. And Andrew? He's doing well also?"

At the mere mention of his name she felt the emotions begin to churn within her once more.

"He's . . . fine."

"The business. I hear you turned the place around! He was happy then?"

"Yes. He was happy."

"Fine, fine."

Trenton cocked his head slightly and stared her down in a way that made Vic squirm in her seat.

"What is it, Victoria?"

"What do you mean?"

"Are you alright? Is there something troubling you?"

"No," she answered with a sigh. "I'm just tired. Listen, I've got a briefing in a few minutes, do you want to sit in?"

"That won't be necessary. You'll do fine on your own."

"Alright then. I'll see you later."

Vic rose from the chair and headed for the door.

"You're sure you're okay, Victoria?"

Flashing a smile in Trenton's general direction, she nodded. "Yes. I'm just great. Why don't we have lunch sometime this week."

"Mention it to Martha on your way out."

"I will."

Pretending to be peachy was absolutely exhausting, Vic discovered. She made a mental note to work on her conciliatory expressions before the elevator took her back down to the 23rd floor for her meeting. All of these questions were really getting to be annoying.

Drew watched Louie as he playfully galloped along the shore, wishing he could drum up even a tenth of his boundless energy. If it had been up to him, he might not have bothered to climb out of bed over the last week since Vic had left. But there was Louie to think about, and the non-stop ringing of the office phones.

She had done what she promised she would do, and he was having trouble keeping up with all of the requests for information. Luckily, the temporary secretary he'd brought in was taking care of most of it, and Tiffany would be back from her honeymoon in two days. It couldn't be soon enough for Drew.

He pulled the square velvet box out of his pocket and creaked it open for another look. Standing tall in its platinum setting, the emerald-cut diamond sparkled in the morning sun, glittering with promises the ring would never have the opportunity to deliver. Drew plucked it from the case and placed it carefully into his palm.

What a fool he had been to ever have put any stock at all in the hope that the small circle in his hand could have changed anything. Vic's future had been all mapped out long before she ever strolled into his life and, except for a short stretch of diversionary bliss, she'd kept straight to her course. By this time, she would be well-situated in her spacious corner office with her name engraved on the door. Why, by now she'd probably forgotten all about Florida and everything else that came with it.

Including me.

Louie trotted up beside Drew and sat down dutifully at his feet. Casting a sad glance over his shoulder, he yelped out one commiserative bark then stared out at the water with his ears tipped attentively forward, as if he were expecting someone to come swimming to shore.

"She won't be coming back, Lou," Drew told him as he scratched the center of the dog's head. "Sorry."

Louie whined slightly in reply, then lowered himself to the ground, propping his chin over his outstretched paws.

"I know. Me too."

Drew placed the ring back into its box and closed it for what he vowed would be the final time. Victoria Townsend had moved on with her life, and it was about time he got on with his. Tucking it back into his pocket, he gave the box a pat and left it there.

He produced the familiar, battered sheet of folded paper from his other pocket and ironed it flat on his knee with the back of his hand.

His eyes skimmed over the e-mail, although his heart had already memorized every word.

> Some things, no matter how lovely for a moment, were just never meant to be. I'm afraid that we were one of those things. But I'll never forget you, Drew. Thank you so much for everything.
> Much love, Victoria.

Drew folded the paper at its creases and then slowly tore it in half. After a moment's thought, he gave it another tear, and then another, until all that was left was a handful of remains that he dropped into the metal can on his way home.

"Come on, Lou!"

Louie scurried to catch up with him, then happily passed him by. By the time Drew rounded the corner of the parking lot, the dog was already up the stairs and waiting for him; just outside the first door on the left.

"Wrong door, buddy. No one's home there."

Chapter Seventeen

"**O**kay, that's it then, folks. We'll have an update on the billboard art by Monday morning, and I'll see you all at the staff meeting Tuesday at two. Have a good weekend."

As her team disbursed, Vic drained the last swallow from her bottle of water and pitched it into the trash.

"How are things going, my dear?"

She shot Trenton a friendly smile as he approached her, and then set about gathering the graphs and notes scattered around her on the conference table.

"I think we've got the deadline nailed on the Rolling Rock account," she told him. "We should have initial artwork ready on Monday."

"Excellent. And when do they fly in?"

"End of the week. We'll have it all sewn up by then."

Her belongings loading down both arms, Vic shifted to one foot and then the other, eager to tie up the conversation and get back to her office. But Trenton appeared to have nowhere else to be, and she suppressed a groan when he pulled up a chair and sat down adjacent to her at the conference table.

"Sit down for a minute, Victoria."

"You know, I really do have to get back to my office. Krissy's arranging a conference call with Joe DePaiva, and—"

"This will only take a moment." Trenton was insistent. "Sit down."

She'd been up against that expression before and lost, on many occasions. Deciding to give up the fight up front, Vic stacked her paperwork on the table in front of her and took her seat.

"What's up?"

"You've been back with us nearly a month, and you've dodged my invitations to lunch and dinner half a dozen times."

"Oh, no," she was quick to reply. "I'm not dodging you, Trenton. But this is a big job you've given me. I want to give it everything I've got."

"No one has ever seen anything less out of you, Victoria. You always give your best."

"Well . . . Thank you."

"I thought you might be interested to hear that I spoke with Andrew Nolan yesterday."

Vic's heart stopped for a moment, and she was just about to give it a hearty punch to get it going again when it began to pound hard against her chest.

"Really? How is Drew?"

"He seems to be doing very well. He tells me you caused quite a stir with the overhaul you made to his business."

"Not an overhaul really," she stated. "Just a little re-direction."

"Nevertheless, it seems to have done the trick. Things are really looking up, thanks to you."

"I'm happy to hear that," she told him, standing up and gathering her things once more. "But I really have to be getting back to my office. Krissy will send out a search party any minute."

"In fact," Trenton continued, as if she'd never interrupted, "he's been offered a very sweet deal."

Vic refocused on Trenton abruptly and held his eyes for a long moment before speaking. "What do you mean, a sweet deal?"

"Allied Corporations has offered to buy him out."

She dropped to her seat again, still holding the armload of paperwork.

"ACI?" she repeated. "That's ridiculous. They're a huge conglomeration. They'll turn Romantic Overtures into a machine. Surely, Drew isn't thinking of selling to them?"

"Well, I don't think romance and weddings are exactly up the boy's alley, my dear. And he stands to make a pretty penny by selling to such an illustrious corporation."

"Yes, but the beauty of Drew's business is that it's personalized. It's unique in that he caters to the individual needs of each and every one of his clients. He's re-invented the wheel there. Why would he want to sell to . . . to . . . Firestone?"

"Perhaps you should give him your input then before he makes his final decision."

Vic felt her heart stop again for a moment. Her first inclination was to rush back to her office and pick up the phone to give Drew a piece of her mind! What was he thinking, after all their hard work to make Romantic Overtures into something special? But then she thought better of it and sighed with resignation.

"It's his business," she managed to say. "I suppose it's his decision."

"Yes," Trenton agreed as he rose to his feet. "I suppose it is. Will you come to dinner soon?"

"Yes, I will."

"I'm going to hold you to that, Victoria."

"I will, I promise."

Vic was so preoccupied with the news she'd just heard from Trenton that she forgot to push the button for her floor when she boarded the elevator, and ended up having to ride it back down again. Drew had admitted to not caring much about the business to begin with, but sell it to ACI? That was like selling a gourmet restaurant to the CEO of McDonalds, for heaven's sake.

As she rounded the corner to her office, her attention was suddenly seized by a set of incessant giggles, one of which she knew most certainly belonged to Krissy. And if she didn't know better, she'd have sworn the other voice belonged to—

"Vic! It's so great to see you!"

The paperwork in her arms slammed hard into her chest with the impact of Tiffany's enthusiastic hug, and Vic gasped.

"Tiffany? What are you doing here?"

"Walter was sent up here for a convention, and I convinced him to bring me along." Crinkling up her nose as if she were imparting some great international secret, she added, "We're staying at The Plaza!"

"That's . . . great. Let me put these things down. Come into my office."

"Okay. I'll talk to you more when we're through catching up, Krissy," Tiffany said excitedly. As she followed Vic through the office door bearing her name, she added, "I absolutely love Krissy! She's a doll."

Vic grinned as she laid down her belongings on the credenza.

"I'm happy to see the two of you in one place," Vic teased. "After I met you, I'd begun to wonder if you weren't something like Superman and Clark Kent. You look entirely different, but I had a suspicion you were the same person."

Tiffany nodded seriously. "The minute I met her, it was instant." Snapping her fingers, she added, *"Compadres."*

"Now there's a scary thought."

"Vic, this place is unbelievable," she said, looking around at her surroundings. "This is like the Oval Office or something."

"Have you ever been to the Oval Office?" Vic countered. "I'm sure it's much more impressive than this."

"Walter said he'd take me one day. I want to do one of those tours and see the White House and the Smithsonian and all that. Oooh, and I saw this thing on the Travel Channel about Vermont! I'd love to go there. Did you know they make maple syrup there?"

Vic sat down in her chair and leaned back into the leather as Tiffany went on at 90 miles per hour. She hadn't changed one bit, except for the purplish tips of her spikey, short platinum-blond hair, and the new tiny braided ring through her nose.

"Listen," she was saying when Vic picked back up on the wings of her one-sided conversation, "Walter's going to be at that stupid convention until late tonight, so Krissy's coming over to the hotel and we're going to watch movies on cable and have something to eat. You have to come, too!"

"Oh, Tiffany, I'd love to but   "

"I don't want to hear your lame excuses, Vic. I'm only here for one more day, so you can't just blow me off and not spend any time with me. We're meeting in my room at eight. You'll be there."

"Eight?" she asked, after giving it a moment's thought.

"Wear something comfortable. We'll just be hanging out and talking girl talk. It'll be like a slumber party."

Vic had never been to a slumber party in her life, but she nodded as if she knew what to expect and agreed to arrive at The Plaza at 8:00.

She listened intently as Tiffany and Krissy said their temporary goodbyes, and marveled at the way the twosome had become instant friends. She'd never given any real thought to socializing with her mop-topped assistant before; she didn't even know how wise it would be, but somehow she found herself eager with anticipation.

A girls' night out? She'd heard of those, but had never actually experienced one. This might be fun after all.

The three of them were sitting in a circle on the floor in front of the television; a bowl of tortilla chips sat between them, as well as assorted packages of cupcakes and cookies, candy and sodas. It was like something out of one of those summer teen movies. She'd never actually seen one, but she'd caught the trailers on television from time to time.

"If anything about this evening makes it through the doors at Marchant, you're fired. Do you hear me?"

"Hey. That's only the third time you've fired me since you came back! Vic, I think you're mellowing in your old age."

"That's enough out of you."

"Yes, Miss Townsend."

"Hey!" Tiffany interjected excitedly, jumping onto her knees. "You know what would make this perfect?"

"Ordering a pizza?" Vic answered hopefully.

"That. And if Drew were here."

Vic felt the expression on her face drop, as if she'd been made of wax and a blast of pure heat had suddenly been shot directly into her face.

"I think he really misses you, Vic."

She stared Tiffany down for a moment, then turned her gaze toward the floor.

"He's very cagey about it, of course, because that's the way Drew is. But I can tell. He misses you."

"Hand me the ginger ale. I need a refill."

"And I just hate that woman from AFI," Tiffany added, passing her the container.

"ACI," Vic corrected. "What woman?"

"Her name is Judith. And she's such a . . . *prude*-ith."

Krissy giggled, and Vic couldn't help it; she laughed, too.

"She's so . . . Oh, *Aaaan*-drew, I think you're going to be so happy with the deal we're making. When you put your Joe Schmoe on the dotted line, we just *haaaaave* to go out and celebrate."

Vic was silent as Krissy dropped cubes of ice into her glass from the bucket balanced on her knee.

"I think he really wishes you were there to tell him what he should do."

"Don't be ridiculous. He never wanted me there to begin with, telling him what to do with his business. I'm sure he doesn't want me now."

"No," Tiffany objected eagerly. "I heard him ask Pen if she thought he should call and talk it over with you."

Vic froze. "You did?"

"Yep. And Pen told him yes, she thought he should." Tiffany's face dropped suddenly. "But I guess he didn't do it."

"No, he didn't," she said stoically, then sliced open another package of cookies with her fingernail.

"Maybe you should call him."

Krissy's suggestion had been voiced so quietly that it took a moment for it to register with Vic, and she glared at her over a mouthful of crunchy chocolate chip cookie.

"Well, I'm just saying."

Vic shook her head and swallowed the crumbs still in her throat. "I'm not going to call him."

"You know what you should do," Tiffany said casually, as if her full concentration were really on the ginger ale she was pouring into Vic's glass. "You should go down there."

Vic nearly choked on the thought, sputtering and coughing until Krissy handed her a napkin.

"No, I mean it. He really needs you, Vic."

"Tiffany, please."

"No, he does. He's just too proud to call and tell you that. He told Pen that you would know just how to handle these corporate types, like that *Juuuu-dith.*"

"He did?"

"Yes. He did. He's out of his element."

"Yes, but—"

"I could make the plane reservations for you right now," Krissy was quick to suggest. "It wouldn't take five minutes."

"No," Vic commanded, then reached for her temples. It was probably just a sugar high, but it had suddenly felt as if her head were about to topple off her shoulders. "Can we order a pizza? I need something to counteract all these sweets."

"I'm just saying. It's the weekend, after all. You could be down there and back before Monday."

"Forget it."

"Okay. If that's your final word."

"It is."

"Alright then."

"Alright," she nodded dramatically. "I'm not going."

"Right. Not going."

They all sat in relative silence for several beats before Tiffany turned to Krissy and asked, "Pepperoni and mushroom?"

The inside of her mouth tasted like something had gone traipsing through it while she slept, and her head was pounding out the echoing beat of the march.

"Miss Townsend?"

Vic's eyes fluttered open, and she jumped to find a complete stranger leaning over her.

"Y-yes?"

"Miss Townsend, we'll be landing in about ten minutes. I need you to raise your seat and fasten your seatbelt."

"What?" she asked, looking around her for clarification.

"Raise your seat, please?"

"Oh, phooey."

Krissy's smiling face shone back at her from the next seat, and Vic shook her head as if she were able to bounce the fog from her brain by doing so.

"We're almost there," Krissy said excitedly.

Vic pulled her seat upright and hurriedly scooted toward the window to look out. The blue-green Gulf shimmered its welcome from below, and the border of land next to it was clearly Tampa Bay.

"Aren't you excited?" Krissy asked her after she slammed back against the foam seat and groaned.

"I can't believe I'm doing this."

"It will be fine."

The previous night was somewhat hazy, but Vic was able to pull snippets of it into her coherent memory. She blamed the near-sugar coma for her current situation, and then quickly added Tiffany and Krissy to the top of the list.

Over the course of a couple of hours, they had been able to convince her that a quick weekend trip to Florida was a good idea. Drew needed her, they said. And besides, wouldn't it be great to see him again?

"Get some sleep," she remembered Krissy telling her after they'd shared a cab from The Plaza. "I'll go home and pack some things, and then come back here and get your bag together. I'll spend the night, and we'll go to the airport together first thing in the morning."

When Krissy had coaxed her out of bed and into the shower that morning, she'd been quite convincing in her repeated affirmations that Vic was doing the right thing.

"I think it's so great the way you're willing to be there for him when he needs you," she'd said as she ran a brush through Vic's wet hair. "He might make a horrible mistake without you there. After all, you know just how to handle those Judith types with their fast talk and their sign-on-the-dotted-line-before-you-know-what's-hit-you schemes."

The thought of Drew selling Romantic Overtures had spurred her on, and Krissy had kept talking until Vic actually found herself backing the preposterous idea. She'd nearly chickened out at the airport, despite the drum roll of excitement inside her at the thought of seeing Drew again, but Krissy had been right there to say all the right things as she guided her down the tarmac and onboard the plane.

"You conspired against me," she accused Krissy quietly without looking at her.

"Who?"

"You and Tiffany."

"We did not."

"Yes, you did."

"We merely pointed out that you and Drew are friends. When a friend needs you, you go to them. That's what friends do."

"You are so fired."

"Alright. But you're going to want to hire me again when you see how well this turns out."

"Oh, no," Vic replied, turning completely in her seat to face her seriously. "You're fired for the rest of your natural-born life. Do you hear me?"

"Yes. I hear you. Now buckle your seat belt. We're getting ready to land."

Vic tried to calm herself with the reminder that Krissy and Tiffany were right about one thing: Drew was in over his head with ACI. Would it appear so terrible that she'd come down to help him with the deal? If she couldn't talk him out of it, and she was certainly going to try, the least she could do was sit in on the negotiations. After everything they'd accomplished together, after everything they had been to one another, albeit temporarily, surely she could give him that.

"Why didn't you just pick up the phone, or send me an e-mail?" she imagined him saying when she showed up at his door.

She realized she had no answer for that one.

Vic followed Krissy down the ramp and into the terminal, shifting her carry-on to the opposite shoulder as they boarded the tram. Her head was throbbing to the exact rhythm of her footsteps, and her ears were plugged from the flight. What was it about Florida that always seemed to make her crave a cigarette so badly?

"Where are you going?" Krissy asked when she headed straight out the doors.

"There's a van out front. We have to rent a car."

"No, we don't. Tiffie called ahead. Penelope's picking us up outside of baggage claim."

"Oh no."

Penelope? There would be no diverting from the course now!

"It's so good to see you again," Pen beamed, wrapping Vic into a friendly embrace. "And you must be Krissy."

"Good to meet you."

The three of them climbed into Penelope's station wagon, and Vic was silently grateful that Krissy kept the conversation light from the back seat, chatting about the flight and commenting on the beautiful view as they drove across the Howard Frankland Bridge.

Once they were across, Vic's pulse began to accelerate, and she felt as if she might throw up.

"Listen, Penelope," she began, then swallowed hard around the dry places in her throat before continuing. "Maybe this isn't such a good idea."

"Don't be silly. Of course it's a good idea. Drew will be thrilled to see you."

"He doesn't know I'm coming then?"

"No, I thought it would be a nice surprise."

"Oh . . . my."

"I'm sure he'll be touched that you cared enough to fly down here when you heard what he was facing. He's a smart boy, but a bit of a fish out of water when it comes to negotiations and things of this magnitude."

"But . . . maybe I should check into a hotel first, and then give him a call."

"You'll do nothing of the kind. We'll go straight out to the house."

"The house?" Vic turned and looked at Penelope seriously.

"Oh, yes, you didn't know. He's moved into his family's house."

"He did? When did that happen?"

"A couple of weeks ago. He's been working on the deck, and painting the upstairs bedrooms. It's such a lovely old place."

"Yes, it is," she commented. "What else has changed since I left? What's Drew . . . been up to?"

"Why don't I let him fill you in on all the details," Penelope suggested sweetly. "You two have a great deal to talk about."

We do? I thought everything had pretty much been said already.

"Krissy, are you from New York originally?" Penelope inquired, and Vic was glad for the change of topic.

"Oh, no. I grew up in Rhode Island. I moved to New York to go to school, and then ended up staying and working for Marchant."

"You like city life then."

"No, not really. It's just where the job was. I'd move somewhere like this in a heartbeat!"

And speaking of heartbeats, Vic's was rolling along at twice its normal pace.

Chapter Eighteen

The heat didn't seem so bad to Vic this time around, and she wondered if it had turned cooler in the month or so that she'd been away. However, as she rounded the side of Drew's house and spotted the silhouette of his form on the hill beneath the banyan tree, a gloss of perspiration misted her skin and a flush of warmth moved solidly through her.

She stood at the bottom of the hill and watched him for a moment. He was as beautiful as she remembered, and she reveled in the opportunity to take him in.

He was bare-chested, and the waistband of his denim jeans hung low. He paused from his work, leaning on the shovel he was using to dig a hole, presumably for the large flowering shrub he'd freed from the black pot overturned beside it. He swiped at the sweat on his forehead, skimming his hair back from his face with both hands, and Vic smiled when his sandy mane fell stubbornly back down to his brow.

Louie jumped up from his nap beneath the tree and tilted his head as he watched her for a moment. She expected his peel of barks to announce her presence at any moment; instead, he set out at a full and silent run toward her.

She knelt down to greet him, and he whined happily as he licked her face and rubbed her cheek with his own. She looked up at Drew, back to his work and still unaware of her presence, wondering if he would be as happy to see her.

"Florida heat," she finally called out to him. "It's annoying, isn't it?"

Drew turned toward the sound of her voice and stared her down with no change in expression. Then he blinked, and cocked his head slightly to the side.

"Not nearly as annoying as women who disappear in the dead of night," he returned. "But maybe that's just me."

Vic took the hill slowly, closing the distance between them, then stopping when the gap was reduced to just a few feet. Louie sat down next to her in a show of support.

"What are you doing here?" he asked her, pulling a wrinkled chambray shirt down from a nearby tree limb and slipping into it without bothering to close the buttons.

"I heard you might need me," she said with a shrug that was much more casual than she truly felt.

"Since the day you left."

Vic lowered her eyes and concentrated on the scrapes on the top of his work boots. "I heard you were thinking of selling out. I came down here hoping I might talk you out of it."

"You're kidding."

"No," she said with a grin. "Why would you say that?"

"What do you care?"

"ACI, Drew? They're a monster corporation."

"With monster funds to offer."

Vic sighed. She didn't want him to see her disappointment, but knew he had anyway.

"I'll ask you again," he said, picking up the shovel and sauntering past her down the hill. "What do you care?"

She stood there for a moment without following him. He paused at the bottom of the hill and turned to face her.

"It's just a company, Vic. This . . ." and he waved a circular motion with his arm, "this is what matters. It was always about this place."

"I just thought . . . Oh, I don't know what I thought. This was a bad idea." And with that, she stomped down the embankment and walked right by him.

She didn't even turn around as she called out, "Goodbye, Drew."

"Hey!"

She kept walking, asking herself what in the world she might have dreamed she could accomplish by coming back to this place, back to him. He was going to do what he always did. He was going to take the easiest route to what he wanted, and there was nothing she could have said to change his mind.

"Hey!" he shouted, grabbing her by the arm and stopping her in her tracks. "What, you're just going to cut and run? Again!"

"I was always going to leave, Drew. You knew that."

"Yes," he said, letting go of her and placing his hands on his hips. "I did always know that. I just didn't think you were going to leave with just a few words out on the beach and a lousy email."

"We said everything that needed to be said."

"When?"

"Out there on the beach, the night of Tiffany's wedding."

"That was all we needed to say?" he asked incredulously. "Maybe that was all you had to say, baby, but it sure wasn't all I had to say!"

Vic turned her head away from him, and in the next moment felt his gentle touch as he took her chin into his hand and turned her face toward him.

"Why are you really here?"

"Romantic Overtures meant something to me," she said, inwardly cursing the tears that formed a foggy mist between them. "We worked so hard to save it. And now you're just going to let it go? Sell it off like a used car, without a second thought about it? To do what, Drew? Hang ten at the beach? Sip a few smoothies down at The Beachside? Don't you have any greater aspirations for your life than that?"

"Is that what you think?"

"Am I wrong? If I'm wrong, tell me."

Drew puffed out a breath in exasperation, then broke away his gaze.

"ACI will turn that place into something generic!" she exclaimed. "Something ordinary. And there's nothing ordinary about your business, Andrew Nolan. It's special."

You're special, she wanted to add, but she was quick to stop herself.

"If it's so special, why don't you buy it from me."

"Wh-what?"

Drew turned back and planted himself firmly before her, looking into her eyes with such intensity that she nearly lost her balance.

"Why don't you buy it from me. You love the business. It's in your blood. Take it over, Victoria. I'll make you a really good deal."

"I have a job, Drew. You don't. You should be the one to keep it going."

"Oh, that's right. You do have a job," he said bitterly. "How's that corner office working out for you, Vic?"

And with that, he stalked away.

Vic stayed rooted to the spot until the slam of the back door to the house made her jump.

"He is so infuriating!" she told Louie, and the dog seemed to pant out his full understanding.

When she finally made her way up the stairs to the deck and walked through the back door, Drew was nowhere to be found. She wandered through the kitchen and down the hall, poking her head into the dining room, and then the living room, both of which were empty.

Louie responded to a rustle from the den and she followed him in to find Drew's back to her where he stood motionless at the roll-top desk, his head slanted downward.

"I'm sorry I left without talking to you," she said softly, but he didn't turn back to look at her. "I just didn't know if I could bear to say goodbye."

When he still didn't turn back toward her, she padded carefully toward him, stopping just inches behind him and touching his back gently. He flinched slightly at her touch, but Vic persisted, cautiously massaging his back with the palms of her hands.

"I read your e-mail," she told him with a whisper, and Drew turned slowly around to face her. "I know you thought I deleted it, but I have software that downloads incoming e-mails to a holding file. It was there, and I read it."

"Ah, Vic," he sighed.

"You made some really good points," she said with a shrug. "We're complete opposites, with nothing in common to hold us together."

"What about love?" he asked seriously. "Isn't that supposed to be a pretty strong bonding agent?"

Vic didn't reply. She just looked into his eyes, and the depths she encountered there nearly overwhelmed her. She felt the words coming out before he ever parted his lips to speak.

"I loved you, Vic," he said.

"You did?"

"Still do." It was almost a whisper, and he lowered his eyes as if he were embarrassed by the emotion.

She didn't know what to say, and then realized that perhaps there were no words for a moment like this one. Taking a step toward him, she wrapped her arms around his neck and held on for dear life as silent tears began to cascade down her cheeks.

Drew pulled away first, then placed both hands on her shoulders and looked at her seriously. "You thought we said everything we needed to say out there on that beach. Well, I had plenty more to say that night, Victoria."

"Wh-what was it?"

"I had this crazy, lunatic idea . . ." he began, and then fell silent. Suddenly, he reeled around to the desk and reached into the drawer before turning back to face her. "What would you say if I offered to give you the business," he said carefully. "As a wedding gift."

Vic looked down at his outstretched hand and gasped. A magnificent diamond ring sat perched in a velvet box in his palm, and the sight of it caused her head to spin.

"Wh-what are you saying?"

"Ah, Vic," he coughed, and then suddenly dove to one knee in front of her. "I've already made such an idiot of myself, I may as well go all the way, right? Marry me, Victoria."

"M-mar—What?"

"Marry me," he said, looking up at her as if he were in some sort of horrible pain. "You can take over the business and make it into everything you dreamed it could be."

Vic's breath was coming in sputtering gasps, and she turned away for a moment, then spun back toward Drew.

"G-get up," she said with a chuckle that immediately turned to a grievous sob. "I mean it, get up."

Drew rose to his feet and stood before her. "Do you love me?"

She wanted to lie, but she wasn't able to do it. "Yes," she said with a nod. "I love you desperately."

She watched the relief shower over him as if he'd stepped beneath a waterfall, and he wrapped her in his arms and planted a deep and thorough kiss on her lips.

"Marry me then."

"Oh, Drew."

"Don't you want to?" he asked her seriously. "I love you, Victoria. Marry me."

Vic looked at him and began to soften. Nothing else seemed to matter at that moment except how miserable she had been without him. New York and her corner office and everything else that had seemed so desperately important to her before she met him began to dissolve away into a cloud of buzzing little gnats that she yearned to swat from her presence. Life without Drew had been distressing and lonely, and being there with him again . . . It was almost more than her heart could handle.

He loved her! And God knew, she loved him, too. With all her heart.

"Yes," she told him. "I'll marry you."

Drew released a reverberating hoot as he lifted Vic into his arms and kissed her nearly senseless.

"You said yes, right?" he clarified when he set her on her feet again. "You'll marry me."

"I will," she said, grinning at him. "But there are a lot of issues we need to work out, Drew. It's not going to be easy."

"Nothing with you is easy, Victoria. Except loving you. That part is maddeningly easy."

She laughed at that and then kissed him again, this time with purpose and conviction.

"Then you'll keep the business?" she asked him afterward. "We'll run it together?"

"I told you, I'm giving it to you as a wedding gift. Romantic Overtures is all yours."

"No, Drew. You need something for yourself too. You need—"

"I know, I know, a dream," he interrupted her. "I have a dream, Victoria. And I'm going to start pursuing it again in just a couple weeks' time."

"Oh?"

"Did I ever tell you how Penelope and I met?"

Vic considered his words and then shook her head. "She told me you were in one of her classes."

"Right. She was one of my professors when I was studying to be an architect."

"An architect? You never told me that."

"What do you think I was doing with all of those blueprints? It's been my dream ever since I can remember. But then my father died and left me the business, and I dropped my dream to pick up his."

"And now—"

"Now I'm enrolled to go back in the fall," he informed her. "I'm just a year away from graduating."

"Oh, Drew, I had no idea."

"You're not the only person in the world with ambition, Townsend. You just assumed I was, what? Some loser who planned on floating through life without a goal? Without a purpose?" When she didn't answer, he let out a bellow of a laugh. "And yet you still agreed to marry me?"

"I love you," she shrugged. "If I have to make a living for the both of us, then that's what I would do. But I can't go on living without you in my life, I know that for certain."

"You won't have to," he promised her. "But you may have to make the living for us after all. For another year, at least."

"I can do that," she said with a smile as she leaned in for a kiss. "Now put this gorgeous ring on my finger so I can go outside and find Krissy and Pen to show it off!"

Drew slowly slipped the ring down the curve of her finger, then raised her hand to his lips and dropped a soft velvet kiss beside it.

"Oooh!" she gasped suddenly as the thought occurred to her. "I can hire Tiffany, and she can do some of the creative work. And I'll bet Krissy would come down here and be my assistant! I don't know what I'd do if I couldn't fire her every week or so. And you know what—"

"Hey, Vic?"

She fell silent and looked at him seriously.

"Would you shut up and kiss me?" he asked. "Because, you know, too many words are our enemy."

Vic burst into laughter and threw her arms around Drew's neck.

"Not my words, honey. Yours! *Your* words are our enemy."

"We'll hash that one out later," he told her, and she giggled beneath his kiss.